Wade Hammond is fascinated with the human story. Everyone who's ever lived has a unique and incomparable life. Whether fact or fiction, deep in the subconscious self are tales of the unbelievable and the extraordinary, the horrific thoughts we would never broadcast out loud. These are stories the author needs to tell.

To my mom, Doris Mae Selvidge, who passed before the publishing of this book.

Wade Hammond

First Active Shooter

AUSTIN MACAULEY PUBLISHERS
LONDON * CAMBRIDGE * NEW YORK * SHARJAH

Copyright © Wade Hammond 2025

All rights reserved. No part of this publication may be reproduced, distributed, or transmitted in any form or by any means, including photocopying, recording, or other electronic or mechanical methods, without the prior written permission of the publisher, except in the case of brief quotations embodied in critical reviews and certain other noncommercial uses permitted by copyright law. For permission requests, write to the publisher.

Any person who commits any unauthorized act in relation to this publication may be liable to criminal prosecution and civil claims for damages.

This is a work of fiction. Names, characters, businesses, places, events, locales, and incidents are either the products of the author's imagination or used in a fictitious manner. Any resemblance to actual persons, living or dead, or actual events is purely coincidental.

Ordering Information:
Quantity sales: Special discounts are available on quantity purchases by corporations, associations, and others. For details, contact the publisher at the address below.

Publisher's Cataloging-in-Publication data
Hammond, Wade
First Active Shooter

ISBN 9781645756378 (Paperback)
ISBN 9781645756361 (Hardback)
ISBN 9781645756385 (ePub e-book)

Library of Congress Control Number: 2024916128

www.austinmacauley.com/us

First Published 2025
Austin Macauley Publishers LLC
40 Wall Street 33rd Floor, Suite 3302
New York, NY 10005
USA

mail-usa@austinmacauley.com
+1 (646) 5125767

Mr. Dustin ▮
▮ **13th Ave.**
▮ **71049**
▮
▮**.com**

4th September 2024

▮**Publishing Co.**
▮
New York, N.Y. 10032

Dear Members ▮ Publishing Co.

Upon cleaning out my deceased mother's home, I found several spiral steno pads and other loose pages. They were in a place of honor, right next to her Bible. She had lived in ▮. On Thirteenth Ave. all her life. Her name was Doris Mae ▮ and she worked as a orderly in the ▮ Hospital. She saved these journals from the garbage can, there were no relatives to redeem them.

Out of curiosity I read the notepads and now I understand why my mother guarded them so closely, I am sending these journals to you because I feel this story is important and needs to be told.

Sincerely,

▮

Written while in Hospital

Chapter 1

The first thing I recalled was lying on my back and staring at the ceiling. The large rectangular fluorescent light fixture hung directly above me on a sea of off-white acoustic tiles. In just a few seconds, it all came back to me. I couldn't believe this was happening to me. All of this because I told the truth.

Since being in the hospital, I've got plenty of time to write this all down. After being in an induced coma for five days, two operations, and with all the pain and suffering that anyone could barely stand, I feel that I have the right to tell my story. To say my piece and admit my guilt. I was cleared by the judge of any crime.

Copied from spiral notebooks

Chapter 2

My dad was a detective, he taught me a lot about rudimentary law and citizens' rights. Even though I have tried to live my life in peace and with respect, like my dad did, still, every turn of the corner was nothing but death and suffering. I grew up in a middle-class American family. My dad worked for the County Sheriff Department. He was a criminal detective. He investigated robberies, missing persons, and the occasional homicide. He never brought his work home with him. He was always upbeat, joking around, and happy. He would play catch with me even though I wasn't very coordinated or athletic. He played an important role in my upbringing. I now realize his nurturing and understanding prepared me to survive in a world of death, sorrow, and depression. My dad was the shining light in my life until the day he was murdered. A fellow officer was taking bribes from gangs and pimps, and raping prostitutes. My dad compiled more than enough proof to convict this bastard ten times over. This cowardly bad cop heard of the evidence against him and thought his life was over. This piece of crap walked into the squad room and shot my father in the back of the head two times.

This bad cop pleaded guilty and got a deal with a concession of psychological duress and was sentenced to fifteen to life with the possibility of parole. The District

Attorney Office wanted this mess to be over as fast as they could sweep it under the rug. My dad was buried with honors. My mom was never the same. I had just started the fifth grade. Actually, my mom wasn't really normal anyway. I guess today they would call it shell shock or battle fatigue and social anxiety. It had something to do with her parents and their family's life growing up. She would wake up at night screaming and running through the house. It was extremely difficult when my dad was at work. When he was working, I would try to help my mom, to stop her and ask what was wrong, but we would end up on the kitchen floor hugging each other, crying, and her saying how sorry she was.

The one thing about my mom is, she is as beautiful as any Hollywood movie star. I would get so jealous and mad at the men flirting with my mom at the grocery store, or the bank, school, or anywhere we would be. She would say, "It's OK, sweetie, you haven't got nothing to worry about. I love you, your sister, and your dad more than anything." She always called me 'sweetie,' which made me feel warm and loved like only a mother can. After Dad was gone, she finally went to see a doctor. The doctor gave my Mom medications that helped her a lot. Mom got Dad's pension and life insurance payment so we had no money problems at that time. She didn't wake up screaming and running around the house anymore, she didn't call me 'sweetie' anymore either.

My sister was four years older than me. She did girl things so I had little to do with her. She cried the day Dad died but never cried after that. She of course had Mom's beauty, but she didn't have Dad's brains. She was in trouble at school a lot. With bad grades, she ended up getting held back a year. When she got caught naked in the back of a van with three boys by the police, all hell broke loose. At first our mom tried to help her. Girl talk they call it, so I was sent out to play. But my sister didn't listen. She would sneak out of the house at night and end up coming home a couple days later. I tried to talk to her once like a brother, only to have her tell me to "stay out of my fucking life." She never spoke to me again.

During all of this sadness, I tried to not bother anyone about my problems. But now seems to be the right time. I am short and very skinny, and I have light blonde hair. It's almost white hair. Got it from my mom. I got a baby face and glasses. The one thing I have going for me is I got my dad's brain.

As a kid, I loved dinosaurs and studied them intensely. I memorized all of the era and sub-periods with all the species of the first fish to amphibians, and later reptiles. When I read about the mass extinction and the meteor strike, it really got me interested in earth and geology. What started as a kids' game turned into my goal in life. Maybe not digging up fossils but working for an oil company or mining operation was my dream. A geologist gets to travel to exotic countries all over the globe. To eat strange food and meet different people would be a new and exciting life for me.

Copied from spiral notebooks

Chapter 3

I first met Brad when I started sixth grade. He was tall with black hair. Actually, he was the tallest kid in the school. Already developing a muscular frame and a deeper voice. He was the new kid in town. Brad instantly struck up a friendship with the boys that got in trouble and got bad grades. And that first day he targeted me as an example of his ruthlessness.

I wasn't very good at schoolyard playing, so I would sit on the small bleachers against the outside bathroom wall. The sun shined there in the morning and the seats were warm. It also faced away from the playground, so I didn't have to hear all the yelling and screaming from the other kids running and playing. A shadow appeared over my voluminous notebooks, sketch pads, and a small pile of books. I slowly looked up to see Brad standing in front of me. His head was slightly tilted to one side with just one side of his lips drawn up to a smile.

"What's you doing, Whitey?" he said this to me with the side of his mouth that was not smiling. No one has ever called me Whitey.

"Studying," I said reluctantly.

He bent down and picked up my sketchpad, opened it up and said, "Look at all the pretty pictures," and proceeded to tear them out of the pad one by one and throw them over his shoulder. Rodger, Frank, and Trevor all laughed and picked up pages and tore them to pieces. Those guys used to like my drawings, they thought they were cool. Now with Brad there, they were mean and not my friends anymore.

Brad threw all my things on the ground and yelled, "This is our hang-out now, we don't want you around. Get out of here." I got up quickly and went over to pick up my briefcase. As I bent over to retrieve my things, Brad came up from behind me and pushed me real hard. I put my hands out in front of me to break my fall and skinned up both of my hands. They all laughed and yelled insults at me as I ran off.

That was humiliating. I never told anyone about that. But now, I knew to stay away from those guys. Rodger was a friend of mine, I thought, and I asked him about it in the class we shared. But he would have nothing to do with me. He said not to talk to him anymore. He was afraid that Brad would beat him up. Everyone was afraid of Brad.

One day I was getting a drink of water from the water fountain and Brad came up behind me. Before I knew what was happening, he put me in a headlock, lifting me up off the ground. I couldn't breathe, I struggled but couldn't break free.

When I was younger and my dad was alive, he would show me some defensive and protective moves. As a cop, he used them a lot. The first was to run, all dads say that, but when you're really in trouble and guarding against a real threat of injury, one must take action. That's exactly how he said it, and I mean the exact words he used. I remember because right when he said it, he grabbed my thumb, just my thumb, and stepped behind me and very gently pulled my thumb back toward the back of my hand. Damn that hurt. Try it on your own thumb, just a little pressure and it's painful. If someone grabs your throat or neck or shirt collar or hair, don't pull away, lean in toward their body and with your whole hand, grab their thumb. Pull it back toward the back of their hand and pivot around to their back. And that's exactly what I did. I could not run away, and my vision was starting to fade, so I had to defend myself. My dad's words came to me and they were crystal clear: "Grab the thumb."

Brad had me in a headlock so I put my right hand on his arm and slid my hand down till I felt his hand. My fingers worked their way up and around till I had the thumb and hooked all of my fingers around his thumb. This was lunch recess so everyone was out of class. This particular water fountain was right outside the multi-purpose room where we would eat our lunch. In other words, there were a lot of kids watching this happen. I was slowly blacking out, so I pulled Brad's thumb back hard. He screamed like a little girl and instantly dropped me. As my feet hit the ground, I still had Brad's thumb in my hand. Still screaming, Brad dropped to his knees. I stepped around him, swinging his arm and thumb with me. Still screaming, Brad tried to turn and raised his left arm. I applied more pressure to his thumb and yelled at him to stop and don't move! He obeyed. Then it just came out of my mouth. "Now say you're sorry!" I yelled at the back of his head, at the same time applying a little more pressure to the thumb.

Snot ran out of his nose, spittle flew from his mouth as he screamed, "I'm sorry!" with a little cry at the end.

All of this took place in a matter of seconds. But within that very short amount of time and with so much built-up anger and frustration, I could not stop myself.

Another defensive move in a fistfight is to not use your fist, slap your assailant in the ear. Another thing my dad would say is never hit someone in the face with your fist. The face is full of bone and teeth, very thin skin with no soft fatty parts. The nose is mainly cartilage but even that will hurt your hand. The palm is padded and has a larger surface, and when it meets up with the ear at high speed, it knocks a person out cold. When I let go of Brad's thumb, my left arm was already slicing through the air. My palm hit flat to the side of his head, right on his ear and the sound of the slap was heard by everyone, including the two teachers and the vice principal who just walked out of the door from the multi-purpose room. Brad hit the ground like a sack of dirty laundry. The vice principal knelt down and took Brad's head in her hands. There was no blood or bruising, he was breathing and moaned a little. She looked up at me and told me to go to the office. I was still angry, furious, and shaking, but I knew not to say a word. I turned around and walked toward the main building. The teachers were dispersing the crowd and diffusing the situation. I had never been in trouble at school. I'd never been sent to the principal's office. Hell, I'd never missed a day of school or been late for a class. I got A's on all my report cards. I was not a problem student. Brad was the problem student, always starting fights, he habitually badgered, intimidated, and insulted smaller and weaker kids. He had bullied me at least once a day all year. My dad would say that Brad was misunderstood and needed help and compassion. That people like that were actually afraid of showing weakness and fear. That their behavior was a response to internal inferiority and they acted out by projecting their fear onto others.

Well, the hell with that. I couldn't take it anymore. All of my rage and anger had built up in me to a point that my conscious part of the brain blacked out and my primeval mind took over in a self-preservation mode. I did to Brad what he was planning to do to me. Unfortunately for me, Brad would carry out his assaults when the authority figures would not be able to witness.

No matter how much I pleaded, the vice principal would hear nothing of it. She didn't want to hear what I had to say or hear any witnesses, not even Brad. She ruled solely on her own observation. My mom came to pick me up from school. The vice principal told my mom what she had witnessed, and that my punishment would be a one-week suspension. I was able to get my school books and work on the class studies and assignments for the week. She also said that if anything else happened like what happened that day, I would be expelled.

When I returned to school, everyone treated me like I had leprosy. No one would talk to me. Everyone would give me a wide berth. I could hear the talk behind my back. Now the kids considered me as the bully. They looked at me as the bad kid. Brad took on the appearance of the victim. He told everyone that he was just joking around. He said that there was never any physical rough contact between us. That he and Rodger played wrestling all the time and that Trevor and Frank socked each other on the shoulder for fun.

They weren't doing it to hurt anyone, they were just being boys – gee whiz, you guys.

He had everybody eating out of his hand. The other guys backed up his story. They even said they tried to be friends with me but I cussed them out. Everyone believed them, even the vice principal and the teachers. I can't believe that I actually contributed to their story. I never told anyone about the constant bullying and physical pain I suffered at the hands of these liars. Not even my mom.

I was so ashamed of the humiliation and my cowardly weakness. So, no one knew the truth. I can't tell them now, it would sound so lame, and no one would believe me. There was nothing I could do except to crawl into my shell and study geology, math, and science as hard as I could. I needed to get a scholarship to a good college and become a geologist, then travel the world. This would get me as far away from that place and all of these people. I wouldn't let anything get in my way. From that day on, everyone called me "Whitey."

Copied from spiral notebooks

Chapter 4

That summer, I mowed lawns, pulled weeds, cleaned gutters, and a hundred other things around the neighborhood to make money. My dad had all kinds of tools and had taught me how to use them. I kept them clean, oiled and sharpened just like he showed me. I really miss him a lot. My mom stayed in the house all the time. I went to the store with her every Wednesday morning. She was always quiet and sad. Only I could cheer her up. She was so proud of me and my great knowledge of the earth and natural science. She told me she wasn't able to finish school but I knew enough for the both of us. I love my mom.

This was about the time that my sister changed. She got caught cutting classes and skipping school. Mom and she would get into fights. I know my mom tried not to yell but my sister would start and after a few minutes they would be screaming and slamming doors. I wished they wouldn't fight.

So, finally I was in junior high school. Got my own locker with a combination lock. Cool. The first day in homeroom class, I saw Rodger and Frank there too. It all came back to me now, but I decided to handle it by just ignoring them, which they did too. I walked around the campus and marveled at the huge classrooms and library. I saw so many books I had already read. My notebooks were crammed full of their information. I had written many essays and book reports on several subjects during the summer. I spent my lunch period going through the library books, maps, and encyclopedia – this was incredible. It made my little bookshelf at home seem insignificant. After my homeroom class, I had Algebra intro; they wouldn't let me skip up to 1 even when I told them I finished that at home last summer. So I did it again, no big deal. Then History class and after that English. Lunch and study class, then P.E., which I hated. Changing into trunks and jerseys in the school's colors. Then stripping and showering after class. I skipped the shower as it was the last class for the day. Everybody called me Whitey.

It was a long walk from home to school but if I cut across a huge field instead of following the road, like I did this morning, I could cut about a mile off my walk. The far south edge of the field was covered with trees in a crooked line. A water source, the trees grew well in the softer fertile soil and abundant water. I went to have a look. I veered off the well-worn footpath and walked in the deep wild rye grass.

That's when I saw them. They had been skirting the edge of the creek bed following me. I started running. "There he goes!" I heard one of them yell; the voice sounded familiar. I'd been working very hard all summer long so my muscles were hard and lean; I sprinted. Then I heard another voice, deep and mean. "You better stop, Whitey, or I'll make it even harder for you motherfucker!"

It was Brad. And he was right, so I stopped. There were six of them. Brad, Frank, Rodger, Trevor, and two other guys I'd never seen before. Unfortunately, I had stayed in the deep grass off the trail hoping it would slow them down, but now no one could see us easily from the road. Damn it! Brad came to a stop about five feet in front of me. He leaned forward with his hands on his knees panting for breath while the others encircled me, all short of breath. "I got something for you, Whitey," Brad said while catching his breath. And with that, one of the guys I didn't know, came up behind me and kicked me in my upper thigh. I think he was trying to kick me between my legs but missed because I had turned when I heard him take a couple steps toward me. This pitched me forward and I landed on my knees. My glasses flew off my face and my dad's briefcase fell from my shoulder. "Remember, don't hit him in the face!" Brad shouted as he tried to slap me on my ear, but I had turned my head just in time so that the blow hit me on the back of the head. Then I was kicked in the middle of my back, driving forward on my hands and knees. I took another kick, this one right to the ribs. They all started laughing. I flopped to the ground and brought my legs together. They kicked me in the head, the sides of my ribs, stomach, and thighs. They stomped on my back, butt, and legs. Then all of a sudden it all stopped. My briefcase was ripped open and bumped out. "Where's your money, Whitey?" I was rolled over and patted down.

"He hasn't got no money on him," was Rodger's familiar voice. I opened my eyes and saw Brad going through all the compartments of my briefcase, finding nothing.

"Where's your lunch money, Whitey?" Brad said this to me inches from my face, his breath foul and teeth green.

Looking right back at him, I said, "I bring my own

lunch." Brad scrunched up his face, frowning, then hit me in the chest hard. The punch knocked me on my back, and I looked up at the sky. They all encircled me again while I lay on my back trying to catch my breath.

"We've been following you all day. I know where you've been and all your classes. So, I want every penny you have, here, tomorrow, or else you get it all over again, you hear me, Whitey?!" And with that threat, Brad kicked me one more time in the ribs. They slowly turned and walked away laughing and punching each other, bragging to each other about their performance and ruthlessness.

I laid there, watching the wispy clouds slowly float by in the beautiful blue sky. Luckily, they were all wearing tennis shoes that were made with soft material and they got in each other's way, so some kicks and punches were glancing blows or misses. But still, I was hurting mainly in the stomach and ribs. I had to be careful, I couldn't let my mom see any bruises on me. I slowly rolled over and sat up. My papers and books were everywhere. I got up feeling the pain all over me. I picked up my dad's old briefcase and slowly started putting my stuff back in the briefcase. The zipper was broken. After I got everything in the briefcase, I headed straight for the country road. No more shortcuts for me. I was limping a little but I couldn't let my mom see me like that. I just had to take it slow and easy.

As I slowly walked on the gravel shoulder of the road, a county bus went flying by. The stiff breeze from the slip stream of the bus buffeted me. I could see several students riding in the bus. The bus's rotating badge in the window was 632. I had to walk through town, and the bus station was down the street from the grocery store where Mom and

I used to go every Wednesday morning. As I walked up to the bus station's office window, I could see a handwritten sign denoting that students' bus card was twenty-two dollars for the school year with the proof of a student I.D. card. I was just issued a student I.D. card that morning. So I went home and counted out forty-two dollars from my abundance of cash, over two hundred dollars from all the work I did over the summer. No one knew about my money, not even my mom. So, the hell with walking and the hell with Brad!

The bus stop was just three blocks up from my house off the county road. I got a route and timetable chart from the bus ticket office. I was set. The bus was right on time and almost full. As I walked down the aisle, the bus lurched forward and I sat down in the nearest seat, almost falling down. The swift and violent moment of my body was extremely painful. I let out an involuntary grunt as I hit the seat.

"Are you alright?" the girl at the window seat asked.

I winced with the pain but turned toward the voice. She was beautiful. I just sat there and stared at her with my mouth open. "Are you going to be OK?" she asked with true concern.

I snapped out of it and smiled, "I'm OK now, I mean I'm OK now that I sat down."

She smiled back and said, "OK," then turned back to her book.

Still staring and smiling, I said, "My name is Miles, what's yours?"

She turned from her book and said, "What grade are you in?"

"Seventh, how about you?"

"We're in the same grade, how come I didn't see you on the bus yesterday?" she said with a smile. I couldn't tell her the truth, what would she have thought of me. But I have never lied, ever. My dad told me that only a truthful person can tell when someone is lying. So, I told her the truth.

"I walked to the school and back home yesterday and my legs and back are hurting, so I figured I'd ride the bus."

"Oh, well, that is a long way, maybe you should move your briefcase, it's probably uncomfortable."

I'm such an idiot, my briefcase was behind me and killing my sore back, but I didn't even notice that I flopped down with it on my back. I don't know what's wrong with me. My mom told me that Dad thought I was too young to be given the talk about the birds and the bees. He had died before we had a chance. So, Mom and I sat down and she told me that one day I would meet someone who will instantly make me feel happy. I would be captivated and afraid at the same time. That I will probably just stare and not know what to say. I would probably do or say something dumb but it would be something funny and we'll both laugh. "Relax and talk like you and I talk all the time, but, and this is important, let her do more talking than you."

I love my mom so much. She's so smart and strong, and like Dad, she has wisdom that comes from experience and life's lessons whether they be good, bad, or horrifying. And the only way to truly gain this knowledge is by living it and surviving.

Written while in Hospital

Chapter 5

OK, the doc and nurses are here to remove my intubating tube. I've been here three weeks and they want me to start breathing on my own. Oh, so I'm told, it's going to hurt too. The chest tube will stay in until they see more healing of my torn lung. The I.V. and antibiotic drip is in my right arm, the whole blood drip is in my left, along with the heart monitor, blood pressure cuff, and body temperature regulator. I have a urine catheter, a drain tube in my right lung, and my right chest is surgically open and exposed for easy access for my next operation. They put a neat little tent over my open rib cage. I'm telling you all this because, they tell me, there is a possibility I won't survive the next couple of days. And I don't care. Maybe somebody told the hospital administrator that I don't have any health insurance. Ha ha ha, the joke's on them. So this probably is the end of the story. The deeps and buzzing, chirps and whirling of the medical machines, all rhythmically come together to sing me a lethal lullaby, encouraging me to sleep forever. But I'm still alive.

Copied from spiral notebooks

Chapter 6

I could not wait for the bus ride home. As I walked to the front of the school parking lot, I saw Frank on his bike watching me from the sidewalk at the parking lot exit. I pretended like I didn't see him. The bus was parked at the curb, sitting there idling, but I couldn't see Candi. Her name was Candace, but she told me I could call her Candi. Then a bus window slid half-way down and she stuck her head out and said, "Hey, are you going to get on the bus? I saved you a seat!" I waved and ran to the bus's opened door. The second step was a little higher than the first so of course I tripped and ended up looking at the bus driver's shoes. I instantly jumped back up.

"You OK?" the bus driver asked. Everyone was laughing as I found my seat.

Candi laughed, grabbed my arm and said, "That was cool the way you fell and bounced right back up." I couldn't help it either and laughed with everyone else. Frank watched the bus pull out and head down the road.

Candi told me that her family moved in during the summer so she didn't know anybody at school. "Would you be my friend?" she asked.

I smiled and said, "Heck yeah!" then I let her do all the talking. I thought I loved her. She lived four streets over, so I got out at her stop and walked her home. We liked the same books; she liked birds as much as I liked dinosaurs. I decided to look up bird species and learn as much as I could. Riding the bus with Candi was a double treat. I got to spend time with Candi and I got away from Brad and his gang. They still threatened me and tripped me in the hallway or punched me from behind.

One day, the gang was leaning against my locker. I waited till they moved and was late for class. They had squirted mustard and ketchup from the cafeteria through the louvers in the locker door; I had to buy new books. The gang was harassing a lot of other students and stealing their lunch money.

When Brad came up from behind me and hit me in my lower back, I went down hard. A teacher witnessed the whole thing and brought Brad to the office and me to the nurse's station. I told them I was OK so they brought me to the office and asked me what was going on. I let them know about my locker and the other times they harassed me. The principal and the superintendent were in the room when Brad, sitting in the other room and hearing everything, said through the closed door, "You're dead, Whitey."

The school suspended Brad for two weeks and would expel him from the school if he caused any more trouble. The gang was disbanded by me. Candi thought I was so brave. Actually, I did not do anything, I didn't know he was in the next room. I wouldn't have said anything if I had known he could hear me. What did happen was the coach of the football team took Brad and his gang under his wing and taught them athletic skills, wrestling, and weightlifting. What had I done?

Candi and I drew closer together. She made friends easily and I tried too. Only a few people called me Whitey. My grades were straight A's and Mom was so proud. My sister was just starting to get in trouble – smoking, cutting classes. She received a two-day suspension for smoking in the school bathroom and fighting with a teacher. Mom was furious with her and they were fighting, yelling, and screaming.

"You didn't ground Miles when he got suspended in the sixth grade for knocking someone out!" What a mess. I felt so bad for both of them. I wished we could be a family again. I wished Dad was still here.

The school year ended and summer vacation was here. Candi's family went to the coast and their summer home for three and a half months. I had all my jobs to do so we were apart for all of the summer vacation. My sister had to go to summer school to keep up her grades. My summer jobs got more complex, such as fence repair and paint, cleaning out basements, attics, and garages. I kept some of the things that people wanted thrown away.

Then old man Hank gave me his nineteen sixty Chevy pickup truck. The paint was flaking off and rusty. Needed a back window. And the engine was all there but didn't run. Mom said it was OK as long as I got a transfer of registration put into her name. With that done, I cleaned out the garage and pushed it in. I got that truck running in a week, but it cost a little bit of money. When I got the used tires put on the rims, I got it off the blocks and backed it out of the garage. Three speed on the column and the K model which was the four-wheel drive and the 327-cc motor. With the short step side bed, it was narrow and fit in the garage with room to spare. I taught myself how to drive a clutch so I used it just around the neighborhood. Old man Hank, limping down his driveway, saw me driving that old truck around with my paint sprayer, mower and such in the back bed; he gave me a thumbs up and a big smile. I don't think I'd ever seen him smile before. I was working seven days a week, from sunup to so dark you couldn't see. I made a lot of money from working all of my jobs and selling some of the stuff I didn't throw away. At night, I read and studied math, science, and history at a ninth-grade level.

I already finished eighth grade level so I needed something to do. I was thinking about Candi and writing letters to her; there was no phone at their cabin.

I started growing hair in places I never knew it would. And my white hair was starting to turn a little blonde. Mom said she would go broke feeding me and with all the lifting and hard constant work. Mom said I was filling out to be a handsome young man.

I had also started a small project for Candi consisting of an ornithology report plotting all of North American birds' migration routes and compare their patterns with the earth's magnetic fields as they shift from the North Pole to the South, and the patterns of the magnetic fields as they collide at the equator. I hope the patterns will correspond and support my theory that the birds use the magnetic fields as a compass and the shift in the magnetic fields when the seasons change.

Candi had finally come back. I was so happy. I had been invited to dinner with Candi, her new baby brother and her parents, they were wonderful people. Candi's father was impressed when I explained to him what I did on my summer vacation. I wasn't bragging, I was just telling the truth.

First day of school in the eighth grade. My new schedule was to walk to Candi's house and pick her up, then we walked up the street to catch the bus. This year we tried to get some classes together. So we both took the foreign language Spanish class. There was only one class so we knew that we would share it together. If I was going to be a globetrotter geologist, I'd need some language skills. I studied French on my own.

In P.E. class, we started with track and field, where I realized that I was very good at several track activities. I took first place in the broad jump and long jump. After a cross-country run, I heard laughing behind me. It was Brad, Rodger, and Frank. They were in full football gear on the practice field.

"Whitey sure knows how to run away, right, guys?" They started laughing louder, pushing and hitting each other on the shoulders. Even the coach who was writing on a clipboard, looked up laughing. I hadn't seen Brad for several months and it looked like he had grown taller and wider since I last saw him. I ignored them.

Sticks and stones, just as long as he remembered that the school would expel him if he tried to pull anything. Later on that week, as I was running laps, I heard a very loud warning, "LOOK OUT!" Before I could respond, the football hit me in the middle of my back, driving me to the ground. The football coach ran up and kneeled next to me. "Are you all right?" he asked with what I felt was true concern. He helped me up. I could see that both my knees were bleeding.

By that time, the track coach came running up. "What happened here, damn it?" he sternly demanded.

"The guys are just practicing running passing plays, must have been a wild throw."

"Are you sure you're OK?" the football coach sounded really worried. But I knew exactly what happened. As my coach and I walked back to the locker room for first aid, I could hear the football coach yelling at someone. I could hear Brad's innocent voice: "Gee whiz, coach." I sat out of practice for about a week and from then on I was watching my back.

My locker had been vandalized so many times that I had stopped using it. I still kept all of this to myself. Unfortunately, I had made only a few friends. These were mainly the guys I studied with at the library. I had helped a few with subjects that they had trouble with. I didn't give them the answers. I gave them a method, my method, in which to organize the subject into categories then break each category down into groups. Each group could then be classified into a single or simplest term. After you have compiled all of this information, then reverse the method and build an outline or graph. With this method, you will retain a great deal of pertinent details that you have studied.

This can be applied to any curriculum. And this was why I didn't have many friends. Early in my life, I had realized that nothing worth a damn was easy. That truth and hard work should not only be expected but rewarded to all who had been lucky enough to be born with good health, strength, and a conscience. And for those of us to help and respect every living thing. Our reward is the tears of happiness.

I digress. So, throughout the school year I was assaulted many times. Usually in the hallway, when class was letting out and the hall was crowded. At first I thought that the crowded hallway was an area I would be safe in. But after several attacks, I realized that bad Brad's gang were surveilling different angles and viewpoints so that the attacks would not be observed by any teachers or hall monitors. They would also have others walking at my pace and encircling me to conceal these assaults. Just like on a football playboard.

They learned my schedule and knew the hallways I'd use. So, I changed my routes to each class and would make sharp turns or just stop and turn around and go the other way. Brad wasn't physically part of it but I knew he was watching. I used certain safe areas to my advantage, so I adapted and survived the eighth grade.

Summer vacation has arrived. This time Candi was only going to the summerhouse for two weeks. Candi and her mom would come back and take care of junior. I had a new partner in my summer jobs business, Candi. She said she could do anything a man could do. And she proved that the first week. To add to the workload, I had taken on some automotive jobs. Not anything major but tune-ups, oil changes, and other maintenance jobs. In the bed of my truck, I had an air compressor, hand winch, and large toolbox. All of them courtesy of my dad.

Candi cried when I told her about my father. We could sit and talk for hours about anything and everything. But our days were filled with work and caring for our families. Candi worked with me during the day then helped her mom with the baby and cooking and cleaning in the evenings. Mom was home all day, she still didn't go out at all.

My sister had been in so much trouble with school and the police that now Mom didn't fight with her anymore. My sister had to go to continuation school if she wanted to graduate high school. She said she didn't want to go. Surprisingly, my sister and Mom took off one day and didn't get back till very late in the evening. I was amazed that my mom left the house. The next morning, I asked Mom where they had gone. Mom was so sad. I held her as she sobbed. When she could speak, she told me that my sister had made some very bad choices in her life. She had been using drugs and alcohol. This was terrible, Mom and Dad never drank. There had never been alcohol in the house, and illegal drugs were unheard of. I felt so sorry for my sister. I didn't know what to do. Then Mom said I wasn't to tell anyone. That day, they went to the hospital so my sister could get an abortion. It wasn't very long ago when she told me to stay out of her life. I know that she was hurting inside. Mom told me the best thing I could do was to leave her alone. Maybe she'd come back to us and want our help. I would do anything for her. Our family has never been religious, no church or bible. Instead, we all looked up to Dad and Mom for support and respect. And they taught us to respect yourself and all others no matter who or what they are.

One evening, Candi was over for dinner. Candi was helping Mom with preparing the food and my sister sat on the couch watching TV. I had worked all day and just finished showering and changing clothes. We all sat down to a beautiful meal like a family again. I was so happy. Then my sister, out of spite, insulted Candi with a cruel joke that I will not write it down because I was so ashamed of what my sister said. Mom, Candi, and I stared at her without saying a word. My sister realized how shocked and ashamed we were. She jumped from her chair and ran to her room. Candi ran after her and went into her room, closing the door behind them. Nobody ever went into my sister's room, but Candi and my sister were in there for hours. Mom and I cleaned the dishes then sat in the living room and read like we always did. It was late when Candi came back downstairs and asked if I could walk her home. Mom and I had already cleaned the dishes, so Candi said good night to Mom and we went out the door. As we got to the sidewalk, she could not hold her sorrow in anymore. She cried and cried, couldn't even talk, she cried so hard. Once we got to her door, all she could say was that my sister was in such pain and needed all the help and love we could give her. Then she leaned forward and kissed me on the lips. Golly.

The last few weeks of summer went by quickly. Candi and my sister spent a lot of time together. I was so busy with my work and studies that I wasn't very good company. But I had made a great deal of money, at least for me it was. I felt that keeping a large amount of cash in the house was not very secure, so I opened a bank account in my mom's and my name. Now it was a real business. I could accept checks and deposit them in my account. I bought some new tools but still I used my dad's tools for the automotive work. I kept my mom's car tuned and in good order, but she said her eyesight was getting bad, and it was hard to drive. That's funny, she read and watched TV, sewed and cooked without wearing glasses. She never wore glasses. She never said anything about her vision till I talked about the car.

I went to the grocery for her; she made a list. We got milk and eggs delivered to the house on Tuesdays and Fridays. And a newspaper every morning. I couldn't remember her leaving the house in a long time.

Then there's the Gomez sisters from next door. They're Mom's friends and visit almost every morning. They were identical twin sisters, Frederica and Alejandra, but they wanted everyone to call them Fannie and Annie. They were much older than Mom. They had lived together all their lives and never married. They lived in a very big house and a very big lot next door and knew everything about everybody in the neighborhood. They came over in the morning to visit Mom, read the paper together, bake bread and biscuits, and prepare other breakfast vittles, all the while drinking coffee and gossiping about everyone.

Fannie would start a sentence and Annie would finish it. I think it was fascinating and if I had time in the morning, I would stay with them and have a huge and entertaining breakfast.

My mom hung the wash on the lines in the backyard and sometimes came into the shop just to see what I was doing. This was as far as she went from the house. It's just that she seemed detached from life. I saw her stare off into space and at times unaware of her surroundings and her activities. She left her bedroom door open all the time. When I get home, I'd go upstairs to her bedroom to let her know that I am home. She usually was in bed early, and my sister was in her room with her door shut and locked. There was always food on the stove or in the refrigerator for dinner. I ate what was around and then I worked late in the shop.

I was now rebuilding engines; I bought auto parts from the auto salvage yard down by the dumps. I drove my truck there. I stayed on the county road and didn't drive in town. I could not believe the owner threw away old engines. He told me that if I wanted them, I could have them. Some of the engines just needed new bearings, rings, and honing. They were easy for me to work on and the assembly was obvious. I've sold eleven so far.

This is the last week of summer vacation. So Candi and I went to high school orientation day to pick our classes and take a tour of the grounds before we started the school year. The school district had moved the high school to a just completed junior college campus. The old high school was almost a hundred years old and was named after a civil war confederate general who advocated slavery. Also, the structure was crumbling, full of tons of asbestos, and struggled with electrical fires.

The tour highlighted the sprawling new school grounds with a large tree-lined quadrangle, a café which was part of the cafeteria, and a huge library. The science, history, math, and art/music buildings all surrounded the quad. Each building was shaped like an L and had two stories. The library was prominently standing on a small knoll overlooking the whole campus. Administration and school offices were in the shape of a horseshoe and were at the very front of the campus, with the main driveway looping the inside of the horseshoe. A large parking lot started as you pulled off the county highway and wrapped around the north side.

The other half of the campus, or the north side, was dominated by the athletic curriculum. A half-shell stadium worthy of any AAA baseball league. The indoor gymnasium was set up for basketball but also hosted dances, pep rallies, and student assemblies. There was also a quarter mile track with an adjacent building housing a complete weight room. The center track is dedicated for long jump, pole vault, and shot-put. The football field was the predominant athletic structure; it took up half of the north side of the school. That's why the school's parking lot curved up to the north. It served as parking for the night games. The bleachers seats were wide with backrest. The upper seats had overhead covers. Two huge scoreboards at both ends and tremendous steel light poles held a multitude of high-watt light standers. The field was immaculate and the whole place could hold thousands of people. A true model of a college campus. I couldn't wait. And a week later, I was a freshman.

I bought Candi and myself our bus passes for the year, with my student discount of course. It was a brand new city bus so the seats were bigger and much more comfortable. We had science and French classes together.

I think I forgot to mention that Candi had been playing the violin since the fifth grade. She was in an advanced music class and once a week had after-school music classes. I had taken an art class since I drew dinosaurs and birds and everyone liked them. After talking to the auto shop teacher about my engine work and automotive business on orientation day, I decided to take on an extra credit class as a teacher's assistant. I could use the school's machine shop to work on my own engines just as long as I made it part of the class project. The first couple of weeks were new experiences, different flavors and smells, bigger classrooms and new teachers. All of this was just settling in when at my locker one day, I found a note that said I was supposed to meet Brad behind the gym at lunch or else I would find 'katsup' in my locker. The hand-written note was sloppy and they had spelled the word ketchup wrong. A meeting with Brad? I didn't want to start out like this, so I thought I'd go see what he had to say.

The back of the gym had two sets of double doors for the boys' and girls' locker rooms. This was where the football players proceeded to the field before, during, and after the games. Twenty-five feet beyond the rear doors of the gym was the backside of the football stadium bleachers. The two structures parallel each other and were over thirty feet tall. This formed a canyon-like breezeway from the gym to the tunnel that went through the bleachers onto the football field. There was a lot of foot traffic in that area and the boys' and girls' P.E. Teachers had their offices just inside the locker room doors. They didn't want the boys going into the girls' locker room. So I was satisfied that I wasn't walking into an ambush.

I told Candi that I was meeting with some colleagues at lunch and would meet up with her later. After I heard what Brad had to say, I would tell Candi all about it. I didn't want her insisting she be there, or worry about me when I would go. I left early and walked to the library. I left through the north side exit and traveled at a moderate pace. The path was made of crushed stone and lined with shrubbery and shaded by huge Penn oaks. This path curved down the hill then ended at the opposite side of the football field. Because this was lunch period, the area was crowded with students sitting on benches along the path and sitting in the bleachers and on the lush green lawn, eating their lunch, laughing, running and playing in the warm sunlight. It was easy to blend in with all the lunch goers. I had taken the longest way around to end up at the back of the gym on purpose. If I would have come from the quad, it would have taken me about two minutes and I would have walked right into Brad. The direction I had used had taken me about ten minutes, but would put me coming in at a different entrance. Which was in the tunnel under the bleachers in the semi dark, and with students coming and going, I'd walk right by them. I saw Brad and Rodger leaning against the gym wall just past the coaches' office window. They saw me after I had passed them and entered the gym's rear double doors and into the corridor. I was now standing in front of the windows of the coaches' offices. I waved "hi" to my P.E. Teacher, Mr. Vargas, turned around walking back out and waved at Brad to come to me. If he assaulted me, it would be in front of the whole P.E. staff. He reluctantly and slowly came over and acted like he was surprised to see me. "Hey, Whitey, long time no see, buddy." He displayed his half smile with big teeth as he bobbed his head up and down with his thumb hooked in his jean pockets. I mimicked him and called him buddy; he didn't like that. "Man, I got something to say to you that's really important, you dig?" he said as he jerked his head toward the wall. "Let's get out of the crowd." We were standing still in the moving crowd right in the middle of the breezeway, so I followed them over to the wall where they were earlier. In a muted voice, dripping with animosity, he snarled, "You owe me a lot of money,

Whitey, I told you I wanted all your money, but I guess I can let you off if you do me a little favor, OK?" He ended the statement with a half-smile and a tilt of his head.

As Brad spoke, I noticed that he was a lot taller than I remembered. His chest was full and round, biceps bulging and straining the rolled-up shirt sleeves. His thighs stretching the jeans. Just in a little over two years, Brad has almost doubled his body mass. I'd been working hard in that same amount of time and hadn't developed anywhere near that much muscle. I didn't think Brad worked as hard as I did, I didn't think he had ever worked a day in his life. Must've been all the sports training and weightlifting.

"What kind of favor?" I asked, showing no interest.

"Look, Whitey, my grades are a bummer. I need you to give me a little help, like test answers, book reports, math papers, you know. If I can't get my grades up, I'll get kicked off the football team. So I need you to give me the answers for everything, know what I mean...?"

"I can't give you the answers, or write your book reports, I don't even know the test questions. How can I do that?" I said while shrugging my shoulders.

Again, Brad's phony half-smile and little laugh, "Listen here, dork, I can get all of the test before anyone takes 'em. I know all the books that have to be read and all the projects that have to be done. I'll leave all the papers in your locker and you fill in all the answers and write the reports, then just leave them in your locker, got it, dork?" The last word he emphasized with a finger poke in the chest. It was rock hard and painful.

"How will you get into my locker?" I asked.

"I know where your locker is and your combination, 26-36-2." Brad smiled victoriously. "I'll rewrite the reports and copy the test answers, no big deal," Brad said this while hooking his thumbs back in his jean pockets.

"What if I say no?" I stared him right in the eyes as I said this.

"Well, then I could beat your ass, or maybe fuck your little girlfriend." I was still staring him in the eye. I wanted to kill this guy. "So look, don't fuck with me, Whitey, and I'll leave you and your little titty girlfriend alone. Hell, I'll give you a discount on some weed or speed, smokes or booze, whatever you want, just play ball and nobody will bug you, OK, Whitey? There's a white binder in your locker right now, so get to work." And with that, Brad and his gang kicked off the wall and strutted into the bleachers tunnel. As he disappeared in the semi dark, I could hear him laugh and give a rebel yell.

I stood there dumbfounded – truly unbelievable. I felt numb. Brad threatened Candi with sexual assault. For the first time in my life, I was unable to react rationally. I didn't know what to do. This idiot was stupid enough to actually commit such an atrocity. I was bumped by a passerby, which snapped me out of my subconscious. Candi! Without panicking, I briskly walked directly to the cafeteria and to where we usually sat. At first I couldn't see her. The place was packed. Then I saw her standing up waving at me to come over. I let out my breath, and smiled while waving back at her. That was pure panic, I was just about to lose it.

As I maneuvered around a table, I saw Brad watching me. He was standing by the side entrance, half-smile, bobbing his head, thumb hooked in his jeans, he brought up his right hand. Index finger pointed straight at me, thumb coming down like a pulled trigger. He quickly turned around and walked out the door with five or six big guys walking out with him. And I mean big, not fat. Chests, arms, legs, all muscle bound and solid. It took a second, but I realized that one was Frank. He was huge, like a pro-wrestler. These guys were serious and I was in way over my head.

I sat with Candi and her friends for a while, playing it cool. Then I asked her to walk with me to my locker. On the way, I told her everything except the sexual assault threat. At first she was defiant, mad, and challenging. We opened my locker and sure enough there was a white binder inside. It was packed with two months of all future curriculum agendas. We took the binder to the library, went upstairs and found an empty study room. As we were going through the extensive paperwork, Candi wondered why not just get the answers rather than just the blank tests. Which was a very good question, so we used reasonable deduction and came to the conclusion that the test answers were protected at a very high level. The paperwork we had looked like documents that had been taken off the top of a stack of tests with limited security. Other papers looked as though they were hastily xerox-copied. Some had handwriting in the margins and words crossed off like corrections were made before it became the final official document. It seemed that whoever was involved in this scheme would have been a lower-level employee or a student who worked or had access to the school office department.

Any student that wanted extra credit could work in the school's front office or work for one of the many school counselors if they were a B-student or above. They had offered that to me but I wanted the auto shop extra credit for obvious reasons. If Brad bribed a person working in the office with, I don't know, maybe something like weed, speed, smokes, or booze, he could obtain these kinds of documents. If he could corrupt a teacher, he could get a lot more. But Brad didn't have a very good rapport with the majority of academic teachers; he did, however, with the athletic teachers. If he tried to recruit the wrong person, he could lose everything. But if Brad sold drugs to a teacher and had proof, he could use that to blackmail them and demand payment of documents and information.

Now we wondered what we should do. If we turned this paperwork in to the principal, we could be considered the perpetrators since we were in possession of the paperwork. On the contrary, we had no proof that Brad had put it in my locker or had amassed these documents at all. To destroy this material would be the same as not doing Brad's bidding. This could have horrifying consequences. *That will NOT happen. I will do this.* If I could pacify Brad's lack of intelligence and possibly use it as leverage and take some control of this situation, I definitely would conceal my handwriting and anything else that could connect me to this deceitful sham. In doing this, I would not be lying to anyone, but if I was questioned by any authority, I would tell the truth.

Written while in Hospital

Chapter 7

OK, now the doctor's here and has told me that my right lung is not healing very well. The repair and graft of the lung has not helped the adhesion and growth. There is dead tissue around the graft and that could be blocking the blood flow, so discarding the tissue and cleaning around the surgical site should restore some blood flow. The tent, these tubes, and my symphony of medical machines will all go with me to my surgical uncertainty.

Copied from spiral notebooks

Chapter 8

Every summer, I studied for the grade level I would be entering. So, the test papers were done the night after I received them. It would have been sooner but I used my drafting board and T--square to write some short answers in generic block print, all capitals, and my dad's old typewriter for longer ones. I also used my old ink blocks for the numbers and check marks. With that, the binder went back into my school locker and was gone by the end of my last class.

Two weeks later, I was soaping down in the locker room shower when I was hit from behind. Actually, I was hit below the knees which put me on my back. Someone slid on the wet floor bowling me over. I had just a second to glance over and see Frank getting up from the floor of the shower and joining in on the dog pile with me at the bottom. Brad's football buddies punched and kicked as they got up off of me from the dog pile. I pulled myself up and with three steps I was out of the shower area and came to a screeching halt. Standing in front of me was Brad. The half-smile, his head tilted at an angle, bobbing up and down. Cowboy boots all shiny, thumbs hooked in his jeans with several big gold rings reflecting the harsh fluorescent locker room light. Rodeo shirt with pearl button and rolled-up sleeves straining at his biceps. Me? I was naked, soaking wet. My hand that was at the back of my head, where the pain was, came away bloody. I spat out the blood from my split lip. It was hard to take a full breath, my ribs and back were throbbing with pain.

"I told you not to fuck with me, Whitey, now I'm going to have to hurt your little girlfriend," Brad said this in a mockingly sympathetic manner. I stared at him with murder in my eyes. "I missed five problems on my math test yesterday, you asshole!" Brad said this while leaning forward and sneering at me. His breath was foul. He smelled of cigarettes. I could not believe it.

"You idiot!" I yelled. "You're as dumb as a bucket of rocks." My dad used to say this about criminals. "I purposely put those wrong answers in there. If you started getting A's on all of your tests, the teaching staff would know that you are cheating and would probably give you a questions and answers oral test that you would fail, and you would humiliate yourself. Do you know how to spell humiliate?" I said this, leaning forward into his face. Brad's face flash red, veins in his neck bulging, eyeballs twitching in their sockets, his tongue rapidly licking his lips. Then his twitching, watering eyes looked slightly up in their sockets and hesitated, indicating comprehension. I was standing in front of a man twice my size. I was dripping wet and naked. I pointed my finger at him and in a commanding voice, I said, "Say you're sorry." The look of unbelievable surprise crept into his face. "Do it, or you will fail," I said this while slowly lowering my arm.

Brad turned his head enough to see behind him, looking at his football buddies at their lockers. Then turning his head back, he looked right at me and with that old half-smile back and said, "Hey, sorry about that, Whitey. That's a good idea, I approve." And with that, he turned on his heels and walked through the locker room. Head bobbing, heels tapping in rhythm, he looked right then left and yelled, "What the fuck are you morons looking at, get dressed, hurry up, we got work to do!"

After I told Candi what happened, she cleaned the blood off the back of my head and put a band-aid on the small cut while I held an ice cube to my lip. Candi was afraid of Brad, she said he was psychotic. But I reassured her that I would handle him like I did today.

"Yeah, sure," she said while looking at my head and lip.

"You do good work," I said to change the subject. "Someday you'll make a great doctor."

"Physician," she corrected me.

Candi and I were not kids anymore. Our bodies were changing and the hormones were altering our thoughts and desires. We were not stupid, our maturity and intelligence was guiding our lives to our ultimate future. We were open and upfront with each other. We had plans to start and achieve professional lives then plan our future together.

At one dinner, at Candi's house, Candi's father felt that as soon as we started at different colleges, we would inadvertently forget about each other.

"Oh no, sir," I said truthfully. "We'll get married when we're settled in the first year and just live in different states for a couple of years."

Candi's eyebrows shot straight up and said, "Are you proposing?"

What have I done! "Oh, no, no. I mean, yes," I stuttered.

"Here at the dinner table?! That's not very romantic" she said, looking at her plate. Candi's dad started laughing so hard that he choked on his broccoli. I got up and patted him on the back, which got everyone else laughing. And I started laughing with them. This was what is known as the traditional American family. And I loved each and every one of them, but at the same time felt sad about my own. My poor dad, my weak and misguided sister, and my disappearing Mom who had become a fixture of the house, but no matter what, I loved my family fiercely and would defend them with my life. We were just not what you would call traditional.

Throughout my freshman year, I worked triple duty – my schoolwork, Brad's paperwork and the yard-work and engine building. Candi was a fanatic about her violin and would have it with her at all times. She could play the instrument so very softly that the sound seemed to be coming from above our heads. She would play in the lowest section of the quad and fill the space with her hauntingly harmonic compositions. Students and teachers in all sorts of stages of relaxation were slowly absorbing the music.

Once I asked her what was the name of the songs she was playing. Candi answered me while shaking her head, "They're not songs, I'm just practicing my scales. I pick a note and play the scales up then down, and just mix it up with some simple chords. Playing with the orchestra is strict in order and exacting in timing. I feel so free and alive when I play solo."

Candi's two friends and fellow musicians play the viola and cello. They played chamber music at small cocktail parties. She was an A student, spoke three languages and was the most kind, loving, and considerate human being on earth. Our future together would be full of love and understanding that would last a lifetime. I promised myself that my family will be loving, happy, and understanding. Like my dad, I would give my life to protect my family. Until Candi and I finally got through the adolescent portion of our lives, and started our adulthood, then we could set out on our journey and the beginnings of fully developing our minds and bodies. But first we had to get through our freshmen year, which Candi did with honors. She had a solo part in the school's orchestra at the first graduation ceremony at the new campus. The principal, with all the teachers, staff, and other dignitaries, made an announcement that thrilled us all. This campus was to be ours for at least four years, if not more. We would all finish our public education and graduate right there. The first graduating class of '68 was leaving and the summer vacation is just now starting.

I loved the summer months, with their warm breezes and late sunsets. But I'm a realist, so I jump into my work projects with both feet.

I met a carpenter at one of my yard jobs. He was fixing the homeowner's kitchen cabinets. We started talking and I offered him a job. His name was Bob and he had been working on construction and framing jobs. Work was thin for nonunion workers those days so he accepted my offer right then. Seemed he lived with his wife and little baby in the apartments in town. I told him if he got to my house early in the morning, he could have a breakfast fit for a king. That next morning, he sat at our old dining table and could not believe it.

"Thanks to the Gomez sisters, it was a meal truly fit for a king," he said with a huge smile. We left that morning with huge lunches. And we cleaned and repaired gutters, we painted houses and repaired wood siding, shingles, and shutters. Mowed lawns, trimmed trees and hedges. He showed me how to use a skill saw and we repaired the patio flooring and rebuilt the stairs. Bob worked so hard and it never bothered him that he was employed by a kid over ten years his junior. I split the day's take in half with him and told him that he worked harder than I did. This made him very happy.

After almost two weeks of working together, I had to ask him why he always walked to my house in the morning and left the same way.

"Don't you have a car?" I asked.

"Yeah, but it doesn't run," he said, shaking his head. Heck with that, I drove him home that evening with a bunch of fried chicken, biscuits and gravy, collard greens and a mess of potato salad. Bob had an early four-door sedan. It had good tires, solid suspension, and a surprisingly clean interior. After a few minutes, I could tell that the spark plugs were fouled with gas. I put some old but working spark plugs in, cleaned the carburetor and jumped it with my truck and it started right up. Bob was ecstatic and couldn't believe I repaired the car so quickly, then asked me if I wanted to meet his wife and baby. I was a little embarrassed about my dirty hands and clothes, but Bob insisted. The apartment was small with little furniture. His wife had a natural beauty that literally took my breath away.

"Quero presentarte a mi jefe. Su mardre hizo la cena, son muy bena gente. El tiene un caro que trabaja bien". Bob spoke to his wife very softly so as not wake the baby.

He was all smiles and introduced his wife as Maria. I bowed my head and in very soft Spanish, I said, "Hola."

Her perfect smile lit up her face as she said, *"Te gustaria abrazar a mi bebe?"*

I held up my hands and shook my head. So she walked toward me and opened up the blanket so I could see the baby. Her wispy dark hair was almost translucent, her eyes squinting shut from the light, skin so fair and looked exactly like her mother's. And like it always did, it just came out of my mouth, *"Puedo darle un beso a la bebe."*

She shook her head yes with a little giggle. As I leant forward, the baby's smell came to my senses – a human smell. The warmth I felt was on my face. My lips touched the baby's forehead just for an instant and felt the incredible smooth, soothing softness of the skin. As I leant back, my smile was just as big as everyone else's. *"Hermosa, gracias."*

As we went out, I said, *"Adios,"* to Maria and asked if they would like to have dinner with my family, and they graciously accepted.

I never held Candi's little brother because I was scared to death that something would happen, and I couldn't help but feel frightened that I'd do something wrong. Maybe when the child was mine, then the love would outweigh the fear. There also could be a subconscious level that the fear was not the actual physical well-being of the child. Maybe the fear was in me and my ability to nurture and support the child during the years of developing into a good person.

My dad taught me what was right, and the power of the truth. He shared his ideals with me in a way that seemed so casual and easygoing, that I took them on as though they were my own. In a way, his teachings were just suggestions and passed on for me to decipher. If I could emulate just a small percentage of the casual wisdom that my dad bestowed upon me, I should have no fear.

The next night's dinner was a fiesta. The Gomez sisters insisted on being there. It was one of those warm still nights. And so much food. I hollered at old Hank from across the street to come over and have dinner with us. That was the second time I saw him smile. The Gomez sisters told us a story that held us all captive.

So they told us, alternating sentences between one another, that they were descended from the Royal Spanish family. It seemed that their father, Prince Juan, had stolen secret codes and documents from the Nazis. Since Spain was in the middle of a civil war, Francisco Franco considered it treason. Berlin demanded the files be returned. There was so much espionage happening in neutral Spain at the time and by both Germany and Great Britain, that chaos ruled. The Prince smuggled his wife and twin teenage daughters out of the country with the help from sympathetic countrymen and eventually the French Resistance. Prince Juan had disguised himself as a Portuguese fisherman and had hidden a large wooden case of pickled sardines in the hold of a fishing trawler. Only the top of the case held pickled sardines. Under those smelly fish were thousands of gold and silver coins, hundreds of diamonds, rubies, and many other precious stones and jewelry. And the codes and battle plans for the invasion of France.

The French Resistance had radioed to the British Navy's battleship the time and coordinates for the Prince's mid-sea pick-up. When the British Navy seamen were rigging a tender onto the trawler side to take on the Prince, he demanded that the large wooden case of pickled sardines go aboard first. It was in the middle of the night, with high seas, raining with a squall gusting in. The British yeoman at the helm of the tender shouted out, "It's all right, gov'ner, we have plenty of vittles aboard ship!"

The family was reunited in London. The Prince turned over the German documents to the British Government, for which he was generously rewarded. The Prince lost his title and had disgraced the royal name of Gomez. Now banished from Spain, the family set their sights on America. Their father found this land that had rich, fertile soil and was very cheap. He knew that half the land was a flood plain but would be excellent grazing land. His family in Spain had raised horses and cattle for generations. He was an expert horseman and a veterinarian specializing in domestic bovine. With the one hundred acre land deed in hand and a house in the process of completion, he left his family to fight the war with the Americans in Europe. Their father was killed in that war. Their mother inherited all of his wealth, home, and the land we are standing on. Their mother sold the land to the bank, and they sold it to developers, who subdivided the land into sites and built houses upon them. Like this home we were standing in right now and the houses all around us.

We all sat there, silent and not moving, with our mouths gaping wide opened in absorbed attention. What an incredible story.

"That is unbelievable." Again, it just came out of my mouth.

Fannie held out her hand and said, "This is one of the jewels my papa smuggled out of Spain…"

"And this is another," Annie said, finishing the sentence.

Upon Fannie's finger gleamed a magnificent diamond ring, and around Annie's neck hung an enormous diamond necklace. We all erupted in laughter and delight, alarming the baby. Even my sister joined in the cheerful joy. Although she shied away from the baby. The dinner was delicious and gregarious. After dinner, Candi, Maria, and my sister cleaned the dishes and brought out the dessert while the ladies doted over the baby in the living room. After dessert, Candi serenaded us with the sweet music of her violin. Hank excused himself and limped out the front door only to reappear moments later out of breath and with an old guitar. Without speaking, he strummed the strings lightly and Candi followed in, and they played the most beautiful improvised concert that I've ever heard.

Mom made coffee and sweet tea, and we all sat out on the back porch and talked about things to come. Bob and Maria needed to get the baby home. When they said their goodbyes, I asked if they would take my truck home. I'd work on their car some more in the morning. What I didn't tell them was that in the back of the truck was a small table and chairs, a baby cradle, and a host of house goods. Also baby clothes and blankets. We all could tell that they were good people, and it made us feel good to help them. Oh yeah, and plenty of leftovers.

When times are good and life is so joyful, it seems to pass in a blink of an eye. But when doom and gloom sneaks up behind you, time gradually drags to a crawl.

Summer was all of a sudden over. Bob and Maria had become like family. Maria spent just about every morning at the ladies' club, while Bob and I worked like fiends. I was hoping that Bob would continue working during the school year but he reluctantly told me about a construction project to build an airport by the States Capitol. The job was scheduled to be completed in three years. There was housing, health insurance, and possible full-time work after the project was finished. I realized that Bob could make a great deal of money and a secure future. I told him that I knew when a good job came up for him that he should grab it with both hands and never let go. I shook his hand and thanked him for his help and friendship. We threw them a going-away party and showered them with gifts, hugs, and love. Mom and Maria cried together, sharing a special bond that I had a feeling was deeper than any of us knew. My sister hugged both of them, then quickly kissed the baby and ran upstairs crying. They felt terrible for leaving, but we reassured them that they were doing the right thing.

"Adios, mi amigos," we said as their car disappeared up the street. I had made sure that their car would easily make the long drive with all their belongings. They had our address and promised to keep in touch. All good stories have a reluctantly sad ending.

A week before school started, Candi and I attended the orientation day. We needed to pick our classes and get signed up. I drove the truck and parked where the older students with licenses parked. It's no big deal. We didn't need to go on the tour that was for the freshmen. But we stayed and talked to the counselors and some teachers. Candi's counselor said that another high school in our district was closing and that the student body would be joining our campus. There would be over twenty-four hundred in the student's body. Incredible! Candi's counselor wanted her to run for sophomore class president, and I seconded the motion.

The summer's hard labor had truly toned and hardened my muscles. My hair has turned a little darker which gave it a golden color. Candi loved it, saying that I was her golden boy. I have also grown my hair long. Nothing crazy, just well over collar and long on the sides and parted in the middle. Setting my work clothes aside, I purchased jeans, cowboy boots, and shirts of the current fashion.

My landscape work decreased in the winter, but the automotive machine work flourished immensely. Using scrap steel from auto salvage yards and the wielding machine at school, I designed frames to transport the long and short block engines for sale. I also started working on clients' cars for rebuilding their engines. I wouldn't take any rush jobs and only worked on one car at a time. So the money kept coming in.

The school year started without fanfare. I had purchased our bus tickets for the year. At orientation, I was given my locker number and combination, so when I opened it for the first time, the white binder was there waiting for me. In extremely bad handwriting on the binder, it stated: "Don't forget." How could I? The binder was stuffed with test papers, assigned readings, book reports, and school projects, as well as completion dates and timetables for the whole semester. No wonder it was fully stuffed. I just glanced at random pages and found neat and compact girl's handwriting. The instructions ordered me to ensure a grade of B on that test. Others had similar orders dictating grades and ranks. Some were slated for A's. This was very ambitious. Unfortunately, I had been working so intensely over the summer that there wasn't much time for my extracurricular academic undertaking. So, as I studied for my own schoolwork, I was doubling my efforts for the two sets of school studies. I was still using my dad's old typewriter for the lettering and the rubber stamps for checks and X's. Mom seemed to be slowing down. She still got up early and cooked and worked with Fannie and Annie, but when things settled down in the afternoon, she napped or sewed and went to bed early. Anything that made her happy, made me happy. My sister had been, what the doctor calls, "clean and sober" for over a year now but still took her pills for anxiety. She had started taking walks for the exercise. Mom still didn't leave the house. We all had our idiosyncrasies and kind of stayed out of each other's way.

An average day had me up early in the morning. Showered and dressed, I hustled downstairs for a big breakfast, sometimes with Candi. Then we took all kinds of food with us to have for lunch and share with others. My auto shop teacher loved the freshly-baked breads and rolls which I bought especially for him. Candi and I would work on school studies on the bus ride there and back. Our different classes would take us to separate places on the campus. But we always had time at lunch and study class. Candi's music friends and my study buddies all got together and worked on posters for Candi's class president campaign. She won by a landslide.

By the time I got home, I would work in the engine shop till dark. Dinner was always waiting in the fridge, and I would always eat in my room. I didn't think I mentioned that I only needed about three to four hours' sleep at night. When I was young, my sleeping habits drove my mom crazy. But instead of fighting it, she worked with it to help me find ways to use my time constructively. My mom introduced me to dinosaurs, figurines, books, and coloring books. I would use the figurines as models for shading and texture. Then I'd cut out my individual rendered dinosaur drawings from the coloring book. The books I read had drawings of the earth hundreds of millions of years ago. The young earth's environment was very strange with plants and trees that are extinct now. I would draw these bizarre and fantastic scenes of mountains, erupting volcanoes, and the flora and fauna of the period. Then pasted in the scene my featured cut-out dinosaur. My mom was amazed with my drawing, charts, and outlines. This was the beginning of my self-taught study practices. You can be a straight-A student and still be dumb in the real world.

I have known Trevor since kindergarten. Back in elementary school, we played together at recess and joked around. We drew dinosaurs and colored in the coloring books in class in our free time. I would show him my charts and outlines, but he wasn't interested. I tried to get him to read some of my reports on dinosaurs, but he didn't want to. When we were drawing dinosaurs together, I told him to write "Cool Dinosaurs" on the top of the page. When I finished my drawing, I told Trevor that we could put both of our drawings together and start a picture book. I looked at Trevor's drawing which was not very good and noticed that he had spelled the word dinosaur wrong. His "s" was backwards and some letters were in capitals while other letters were in lower case. His penmanship was atrocious and some letters were indistinguishable. I realized that Trevor had some writing and spelling problems. I didn't want to embarrass him so I said that it was great and we started our book. For a couple of weeks, we added more pages to the "Cool Dinosaurs" book. I tried to help Trevor with his spelling, but even when I spelled the word out for him, he still spelled it wrong. He was mixing capitals and lowercase letters randomly in the same word, and his e's and s's were backwards. He also inverted the letters b and d. I tried to help him and correct some of the mistakes, but he would get frustrated and walk away, not wanting to participate anymore. I really felt bad and dropped the whole book thing and just played whatever he wanted to do. Sometimes, he was real quiet, and other times he would start a sentence but stop and not finish it. Other times he would smell really bad like he had not bathed in a while. The majority of the time he just didn't seem to be very happy. No one saw him the whole freshman year. I heard that he was caught selling drugs and was sent to the juvenile detention facilities.

My first period class was Algebra advance and was in the Science and Math building right by the gym and locker rooms. As I made my way through the quad and up the stairs to the Science and Math building, I walked right into Brad who was standing at the top of the stairs. My gosh, his body was even bigger than last year.

"Come over here, Whitey," Brad said this with a jerk of his head, stepping over to a group of trees growing just past the stairs on the gentle sloping hillside. There was a rush of people on the broad stairway and I'd rather not be seen in the company of Brad, so I stepped into the cover of the foliage with him. We were somewhat hard to see in the shadows of the tan oak's drooping branches. His eyes darted back and forth several times then suddenly stopped at the sight of me. His pupils were pin pricks, the acne scars in his face were deep and reddish. His tongue rapidly licked chapped lips, and above them the beginning of a thin mustache. His neck is wide, chest thick, and the roll-up shirt sleeves are straining.

"I want you to come right back here after your class, Trevor will give you something and you are to put it in your locker, got it?" And without waiting for an answer from me, he took off down the slope toward the locker rooms.

Trevor? I hadn't seen him in a long time. They probably wanted me to give him test answers too. Whatever. I had other things to think about. When my algebra class ended, I stayed to hand in some extra credit work. I didn't want any trouble from Brad or his gang, so I walked to the main stairway to meet with Trevor. As I approached the stand of trees, I could see Trevor trying to hide in the shadows. I startled him when I said, "Hi."

He was wearing an old army coat and his hair was unkempt. His cheeks were sunken and he had dark circles under his eyes. He was a mess. Silently, Trevor took two steps toward me and just barely lifted his arm, he said, "Here, put this in your locker."

I couldn't see what he had in his hand, he was cupping his hand to conceal whatever it was. Surely it wasn't a binder or a handful of papers, so I felt a little leery and took a step back. "Take it, god damn it!" There was panic in his eyes as he tried not to yell. I took another backwards step, wanting nothing to do with this.

"You two stay right there!" This command came from the broad stairway and was instructed by Mr. Goff. Mr. Goff was one of the Security and Custodial Staff. Security policed the campus grounds for illegal activities. Custodian policed the campus ground for trash. I remembered seeing him in the lower quad relaxing and mesmerized by Candi's violin. Mr. Goff was very tall and thin. His dark hair was plastered to his head with hair grease and combed over with a severe left side part that was a perfect straight line. With his ever-changing sport jackets and slacks but always the same white shirt and black bow tie. With his horn-rimmed glasses, he looked just like Clark Kent. Mr. Goff was taking the stairs three at a time. It took Trevor a couple of seconds to process his position in his immediate situation. And like a wild animal, he dropped what was in his hand and ran. Without moving, I looked intensely at what Trevor had dropped. It looked like a plastic sandwich bag full of white powder. Mr. Goff put his hand on my shoulder as we both watched Trevor round the corner and enter the boys' locker room.

"I know who that is," Mr. Goff said while bending down to place his handkerchief over the plastic sandwich bag before picking it up. And with that, he led me down the broad stairway, across the quad and to the back of the Administration building. The door we walked through was made of metal and was placarded: "School Personnel Only." We walked down the hallway and turned right. Then right at the next hallway and right again at the first door. Mr. Goff opened the door and I stepped in. He took my books and briefcase, then pointed to a chair in the corner and said, "Sit," which I did. Then pointed at me and said, "Stay," while closing the door. I think this guy had a dog at home.

In just a few minutes, Ms. Hallikamp burst in with true concern. "What's going on here, Miles?" she said this as she sat on the corner of the desk. Ms. Hallikamp is my counselor and a very different kind of woman. She is compact and wears her hair cut short. She wears no makeup and always wears slacks and tucked in shirts. She also doesn't wear fingernail polish but every finger is adorned with at least one ring. She is always fair, intelligent, and involved with all student activities. She is a beautiful person who I trust completely.

"I have no idea," I said honestly. My dad had interrogated a lot of people and told me how he used psychology to win them over and befriend them so that they would feel comfortable and confide in him. Other times, when the evidence was overwhelmingly against them, my dad would tell them not to say anything. "You have the right to remain silent. Use your rights to your advantage. If you cannot afford private counsel, one will be appointed by the court as a public defender for your first court date calling for your arraignment. Make no plea, and ask for a court appointed Defense Attorney. Your first public defender will notify you of your rights and let you know who will be representing you in your case. Tell them the truth." All court-appointed attorneys have a sworn duty to keep conversations with clients completely confidential and protected by law.

A lot of the detectives did not appreciate my dad's compassionate display of leniency. But the county prosecutor never lost a case that used my dad's interrogation technique. Usually they took a plea bargain, plead guilty, and sometimes gave the investigators information about other crimes and perpetrators.

My dad's advice to me was to always tell the truth. Answer all of their questions truthfully, but just answer the question in as few words as possible. Try to answer as many questions with a "yes" or "no." Don't volunteer any extra information. Tell the truth, just remember that you don't have to tell them everything unless they ask.

"I had no idea what Trevor was doing. Not until Mr. Goff was standing right next to me, did I know what was in Trevor's hand. I know as much as Mr. Goff does."

"Miles, there is a great deal of what we think is cocaine in that plastic bag. Mr. Goff is notifying the police to take possession of the evidence and investigate this matter. Now Mr. Goff said he saw Trevor handing you this plastic bag, is that right?" Ms. Hallikamp was prompting the interrogation.

"No, ma'am, my hands were full with my briefcase and my algebra books. Actually, I took a step back from Trevor when I realized how terrible he looked," I said defensively.

Ms. Hallikamp looked at the opened office door and said, "Is that right, Mr. Goff?"

Mr. Goff stepped in, obviously he had been standing in the hallway listening to our conversation.

"Well, he did step back from Trevor and Miles did have his hands full," Mr. Goff said reluctantly.

"Did he ever have possession of the plastic sandwich bag?" She was now interrogating him.

"No, I didn't see him with it," Mr. Goff said awkwardly.

"So, Miles, your fingerprints will not be found on that plastic big, is that right?" she said this while leaning forward and looking me right in the eye.

"Yes, ma'am, that is correct," I said looking right back at her.

"Then why were you there?" Mr. Goff asked authoritatively.

I turned my attention toward him and said, "I've known Trevor since kindergarten and haven't seen him in a year and a half. I just wanted to say hi."

We sat there looking at each other until Ms. Hallikamp said to Mr. Goff, "I know Miles, he's an excellent student, a straight-A student. He would not be involved in anything like this. I'm convinced he had nothing to do with this. He doesn't need to be interviewed by the police."

A uniformed police officer arrived and bagged the evidence, talked to Ms. Hallikamp and the school's principal, then left. I was given my briefcase and books back and was told that I might have to speak with the police at a later day. Of course, I understood and would be available at any time. I could tell that my briefcase had been searched. I was glad that I didn't have the white binder with me. It only took twenty-four hours for everybody in the school to find out what had happened. Candi was very scared but sympathetic. I wasn't sure how to get out of this but I needed to convey to Brad that I will have nothing to do with any drugs otherwise I will have nothing to do with him. I left a note with the test answers in my locker stating that very thing.

One of the students in my study group took me aside and told me about his brother. His brother was a senior and on the varsity football team.

From what he told me, I now realized just how dangerous and illegal the situation was. What he told me was that Brad was a drug dealer and was supplying the whole school and town with illegal drugs, and was blackmailing a lot of students into distributing and selling a variety of drugs. It didn't stop there; stolen cigarettes and alcohol without the state's tax stamp were illegally being sold throughout the county at half price. And finally, Brad was selling a pharmaceutical hormone injected into the body to intensify the body's muscle growth.

No wonder why Brad, Frank, and the other gang members are so muscle bound. When I had written the note about not cooperating with the drugs, I had no idea of the depth of the situation I was involuntarily immersed in.

A week later, I found a note in my locker. In very delicate feminine cursive writing, the note stated that I should continue to complete the school papers and no harm would come to Candi or myself. This was a serious situation and one I did believe was going to be very difficult to get away from.

In just less than two years, Candi and I would be away from there and on our way to a beautiful long life together. I had to shield her and keep her as far away from this insanity. I couldn't tell her any more about the cheating test answers and notes like this one.

The first thing was to stop carrying the white binder around. I could leave it in the locker and put the papers in my briefcase, disguising them with other papers. I would only work on them at home in the evening. Instead of walking through the school with the finished papers, I'd go around the north side to the boys' locker room and leave them in my gym locker. I had my own lock on my gym locker. I could bend a piece of sheet metal like a shallow square tray. Then glue magnets on the edges, paint it the same color green as the locker, and stick it under the shelf in the locker. With the papers hidden inside, no one would ever find them. When I had all the paperwork finished, I'd take them out of my gym locker, put them in my gym bag, and transfer them to the white binder in my hall locker at the end of the day. I couldn't tell Candi about any of this. Actually, Candi is the only person I had told about all of this. She promised never to tell anyone about the cheating school paperwork and understood how crucial it was. And those precautions were proven prudent foresight.

Two weeks after the ordeal with Trevor, right at the end of my algebra class, my teacher casually told me that Ms. Hallikamp would like to see me in her office. I was just leaving the room and the majority of students were already gone, so no one heard her instruction. I answered with a slight but quick nod of my head. The way she lowered her voice convinced me that she did not want anyone else to hear.

I proceeded directly to my counselor's office. I easily saw Mr. Goff trying to hide in the crowd, but never made eye contact. He was watching for my reactions and activities following my counselor's request. I entered the

Administration building at the front doors and asked to see Ms. Hallikamp. I was granted access to enter the office hallway and made my way to Ms. Hallikamp's office. There was a middle-aged gentleman in a suit, tie, and holding his hat standing in the hallway next to Ms. Hallikamp's office door. She was leaning against the doorframe with her arms crossed on her chest talking to the gentleman quietly. Upon seeing me, Ms. Hallikamp stood up and gave me a very reassuring smile. I smile back and confidentially walk up to both of them.

"Miles, this is Detective Hansen, he has a few questions for you, is that alright?"

Mr. Goff walked up from behind me as I was shaking the detective's hand and said, "Sure."

Mr. Goff helpfully said he would hold my briefcase. I handed it to him and asked him to take my algebra book too. Ms. Hallikamp, Detective Hansen, and I went into the office and found a chair.

With the door closed, Detective Hansen looked at me in a serious way. Sitting forward in the plastic chair, with elbows on his knees he said, "I'm sorry to tell you this but we found your friend Trevor dead in the rye fields outside of town yesterday."

"What?" I was dumbfounded.

"Where were you last Friday night?" This was Detective Hansen's first official standardized question.

"About the same as all week nights, I work on a neighbor's car then dinner with my mom and sister and after that homework and then bedtime," I said this looking straight at the detective – the truth and nothing but the truth. What I didn't say was that I had installed a rebuilt engine in a client's truck, said hi to my mom on the way to the kitchen, ate in my room and wrote, stamped, and typed till two o'clock in the morning.

"Did you see Trevor any time after your encounter by the Math building?" Detective Hansen asked as he referred to a small notebook.

"No," I answered instantly.

"Listen, son, I'm not trying to upset you but we have nothing to go on. Your friend was murdered so anything could help." I felt so helpless and hopeless. I couldn't say Bad Brad did it. I had no proof, no evidence. I could speculate with Brad's threats and extortion, intimidation and blackmail. But that was not proof. All that would prove was my admission of guilt and nothing against Brad. I looked at Ms. Hallikamp with self-pity in my eyes that she took as sorrow.

"I can see that you are hurting, Miles, and that Trevor was a friend to you in the past. Why don't you go to the front desk and get a hall pass? You don't need to go to any class. Go home or just relax around campus. You know you can come and see me anytime, right?"

I shook my head yes. Detective Hansen gave me his card and told me if I think of anything, to call this number and he would call me back. He asked me not to tell anyone about our talk for the time being. When the door was open, Mr. Goff was standing there with my briefcase and algebra book in his hands. He was handing me my things and at the same time shaking his head "no" to Ms. Hallikamp. I picked up my hall pass, which would grant me access to any part of the school for the rest of the day. I went to the cafeteria and bought a huge cinnamon roll with a cup of coffee. The cinnamon roll was warm, the coffee strong. Why is this happening to me? Brad killed Trevor. Trying to act normal, I opened my case and retrieved my notebook and some pens and protractor. Under all of this was a stack of paper, some printed and others hand-written. Mixed in with these papers were the test answers for several subjects. Mr. Goff was looking for drugs and other evidence but not test answers. If the white binder would have been in my briefcase, he would have found a condensed version of test answers and test assignments. It would have been hard to miss. Ms. Hallikamp wouldn't have missed anything. If the school's security officer searched my locker and found a note or unauthorized school paperwork, I'd have been caught red-handed.

After my morning snack, I headed to the library and worked on several different projects. After a few hours, I checked out a book and just as I was about to walk out of the library, a very attractive girl came up to me and said, "Hi, Miles."

The library's entrance was actually an atrium. The large glass doors, walls, and ceiling created a room with plants and small slow growing trees placed in stylish urns and planters with sitting areas on both sides. After the atrium, there was a huge stone staircase leading up to the main floor of the library. Because of the height of the staircase, we could not be seen by anyone in the library. With students all in their classes, there was hardly anyone in the library anyway. "Can we have a seat and talk a little?" she asked as her green eyes sparkled and her white teeth gleaming.

"Sure," I answered. "You're a cheerleader, aren't you?" I asked while we were just finding our seats on the stone bench.

"Yeah," she said shyly. "So, Brad wants to know why you are talking to the man?"

She was just delivering a message, she really didn't know what this was all about, but I had an idea. "They were questioning me about a murder."

"Oh," she said, drawing back and wincing.

"Listen, you tell Brad that I know, but I didn't say anything. Tell him my locker isn't safe anymore. Tell him to get the gym locker right next to mine. He can lock it up and put one of the locker keys through the vent louvers of my locker. I'll put everything in that locker where no one will ever look. Now listen, you tell him that I know what he's done! And if anything happens, I know! You got it."

I talked to her like she was a child. Made her repeat everything I had said. Then I shooed her away and waited for a while just to make sure no one had seen us talking. Brad thought that I would be all starry-eyed with this groovy chick and tell her everything. Actually, I was mean and hard on her. And that left an impression, but not a good one. From there, I walked all the way around the school to the shop classes. I got stopped and asked to see my hall pass one time. At no time did I see Mr. Goff sneaking around. I got to the auto shop class and showed my teacher my hall pass, then asked if I could help him for the rest of the day.

"Hell, Miles, you could pretty much teach the whole class, and I appreciate your help." I finished my day and met up with Candi for the bus ride home. I didn't lie, I just didn't tell her about anything. The next day, I went through my customary routine. There was no talk about Trevor's death around school. I did believe that in time that will change.

Right before my P.E. class, I went to my locker to drop off my books and paperwork. Also, nonchalantly, I placed the white binder in my briefcase.

This was when I was at my most vulnerable, there were only a few pages of test answers that I hadn't hidden in my gym locker yet. I guessed my message got through since the binder was still there. I walked directly to the gymnasium's front entrance, inside I kept close to the expendable bleachers because a heated game of basketball was in progress. All of the spectators were cheering with wild enthusiasm. At the far end of the gym, there were two sets of double doors leading down a broad flight of stairs. At the bottom, the corridor was flanked by bathroom entryways, women's on the right, men's on the left. These were primarily used by the public after school hours sporting events. They were spacious and accommodating. The majority of the students didn't use them. The wide corridor ended at a large T-intersection. A left turn took you to the boys' locker room and shower, a right led to the girls. Straight ahead took you to two sets of double doors and outside to the breezeway between the gym and the football stadium's bleacher tunnel. Windows were set inside the corridor on both sides, just before the double doors. Also there were sets of windows outside the breezeway flanking the double doors. These windows were for the coaches and athlete instructors' offices and for observation of the students' comings and goings inside the corridor and outside the breezeway and the tunnel into the stadium.

I turned left into the men's public bathroom. I picked a random stall toward the far end and locked the stall door behind me. Setting my briefcase on the commode, I took out the white binder and removed all its contents. I added all the fraudulent school test answers and reports into one pile. The white binder with the poorly written "Don't forget" on the front had to go. Putting everything back in my briefcase, I left the bathroom and headed to my gym locker. Standing in front of my gym locker, I dropped my things on the backless wooden bench and opened my locker. At the bottom floor of the locker, I noticed a brand-new key. The locker to the left of mine had a brand-new lock. I placed the key on the top shelf and changed into my P.E. shorts, shirt, and shoes. All my school clothes and briefcase got locked up and the key for my locker was on my wrist. After the class, I showered, dried off, and dressed. Then casually I walked away. After several steps, I stopped and acted as though I had forgotten something. I went back and opened the decoy locker. With my briefcase at my feet, I took out all the paperwork and the magnetic tray that was in my locker but now I attached the tray to the bottom shelf in the decoy locker. A small note folded like a tent stated, "Look under the shelf." After fastening the lock, I picked up my briefcase and walked out and headed to my next class. Anyone watching me could not have differentiated my locker from the decoy locker. From then on, I could open either my locker or the decoy locker without any worry of detection. Still, I needed to camouflage the paperwork by mixing them with other innocent papers and documents. If I could streamline my transfer of paperwork and maintain a delivery system, I would never have to speak or associate with any of Brad's gang ever again.

Written while in Hospital

Chapter 9

Time has forgotten me and left me behind. I have lost track of this thing called time. The hospital has kept my room in the critical care ward semi-dark and they won't tell me the date or if it's day or night. I haven't eaten or drank anything since I can remember. I can only communicate in writing because of the feeding tube down my throat. A very nice and concerned orderly has assisted me faithfully throughout my visit here. I sense her feeling of empathy and pity. In her eyes, I see my plight and what is to come. She washes me and helps as the nurses turn me to change the linens and absorbent pads around me. All the disinfectants, antiseptic, and other perfumed cleaning products still cannot mask the putrid odor of my wound and body. And still, she is diligent in her gruesome tasks with a smile on her face and a tear in her eye. She's the one who brought me sharpened pencils and the spiral bound notebooks… At first, when I woke up in the hospital, I gestured for a writing instrument to communicate with the staff. They gave me a pencil and a small piece of paper. When I asked for a notepad, the nursing staff said I shouldn't exert myself. The little orderly, not knowing about the nurse's decision, brought me several spiral bound notebooks and a box of pencils which she sharpened. I let the annoyed nurses know that what the orderly did was a very compassionate act and my writing has helped me to deal with my pain and my state of mind. I was shot in the right side of my chest. The bullet entered the right side of my chest just past my sternum, shattering two ribs and breaking another. Just missing my heart, the bullet traveled at a twenty-degree angle through my lung and out my right armpit, shattering the three same ribs. My right lung was ripped in half, pulverizing the lower half. The doctors and staff are trying to save the upper part of the lung but are struggling with several complications. Removing the remaining portion of the lung could jeopardize the other damaged tissue. When the bullet went through me, it ripped my chest open, leaving the splintered white ribs and red fibrous muscles, flapping against my abdomen. A Smith & Wesson .44 caliber magnum handgun is a formidable tool. Maybe I should mention that I am left-handed and also have practiced for years to become ambidextrous. The only part of my body I can partially move freely is my left arm. I need to finish my story.

Copied from spiral notebooks

Chapter 10

Candi had written an article in the school's newspaper at the end of the school year. There was a drug problem in our high school. There have been three students murdered this year. Trevor was one of them. Several students were arrested for drug related offenses. Eighteen students had died from overdose of heroin, cocaine, and methamphetamine tablets.

Four female students died when their car drifted into the oncoming lane and were hit head on by another vehicle. The elderly couple in the other car were coming home after celebrating their fortieth wedding anniversary. Mr. Mclaughlin was also celebrating his ten years of sobriety.

The four female students had alcohol and cocaine in their blood system. The bottle of booze had no state tax stamp on it. They were all A-students, and one girl was the cello player in the string ensemble Candi performed with.

Drugs were easy to obtain and plentiful. Smoking cigarettes was illegal for people under eighteen and on school grounds, but nothing could be done about it off campus property. The north side of the campus, beyond all of the sports structures, was the county park. Heavily wooded but with some open spaces with picnic tables and benches. Hiking trails led through the park and up into the rolling hills. This was all public land and open at sunrise and closed at sunset. This park had also become the school's unofficial smoking area. But cigarettes weren't the only thing smoked in the park, and that was the real problem. The park had become a drug outlet and a place for users. Police couldn't approach unnoticed. There was only one way to enter the park. From the gentle slope of the hills above the parking lot, the cops could be seen from many vantage points. The dense woods gave cover to the users and suppliers. Some students just wanted to smoke a cigarette and didn't go any further than the parking lot. The police had more important matters to attend to other than writing tickets for underage smoking or running around chasing potheads in the woods. Although anyone found in the possession of any illegal drugs on school grounds was turned over to the police and expelled.

Candi, as class president, took it upon herself to investigate the drug culture and categorize the people who consumed drugs habitually and were exploited because of it. She started a program that gave anybody a voice about the drug problem at school.

In the school's newspaper, Candi wrote an article telling everyone who wanted to tell their story about the drug issue, could leave a note at any table in the library. The library staff would collect all of the notes and save them for Candi. At first, only a few trickled in, but after two weeks she had amassed over one hundred and fifty testimonies. Several friends of Candi and I worked on separating the pros and cons.

There were comments about being young and wanting to have fun and do crazy things, others stating that it was just an experiment in order to evaluate and determine if the effects were enjoyable or unpleasant. They also thought that that decision should be determined for themselves. Though the majority were afraid of the criminal element that it brought into the school and the young lives lost to drugs. A few voluntarily named pushers and locations where someone could score. One note written in sloppy print stated, "Mind your own busines"; the word "business" was misspelled. I knew who wrote this. I told Candi we had to be very careful about the information that had been gathered. I said that this was not our responsibility, this was what the police were for and what we had collected was not evidence. Without witnesses, giving corroborating statements made personally to the police and testifying in court, then all of this was for nothing. Candi agreed that this project was a case study and not an official investigation. But if she could help just one person then all of this was worth it.

Within two months, Candi had accumulated so much data that she wrote another compelling article in the school's newspaper. Some of her exact verses were, "The law is our moral compass and exists to protect the safety and the rights of all people. If we, as a society, do not agree with these laws, then we cast ballots and the people reach decisions by voting. This fills the requirements as our intellectual and sophisticated future advances."

Then Candi turned the sharp tip of the sword toward herself and confessed to her addiction of being enslaved into a psychological and physical habit to which causes severe trauma if separated or kept away from her violin.

Candi's violin was always by her side. She woke in the morning with the instrument in bed with her. The old violin needed to be stored in a warm environment. Candi's body. It was right by her side at the breakfast table, right by her side all day at school. And with her in the evening until she went to bed. During all that time that the violin was by her side, she was constantly playing it every chance she got. For just a few minutes before class, or an hour at lunch.

Candi's father found this violin in Italy. A small museum in Rome had displayed a Stradivari for over one hundred years. New technique with powerful microscopes that use different light sources, discovered that the violin was not a Stradivari but it was a Vuillaume made two hundred years later. Jean Baptiste Vuillaume was one of the finest violin makers in France. He started training when he was a teenager and by 1828, started his own studio where he manufactured, taught and sold violins of many designs. Vuillaume experimented with many of Stradivari's building techniques and lacquer formulas. Imitating Stradivari's design so perfectly that scientists accidentally identified a Vuillaume as a Stradivari.

The scientists all agreed that the instrument was manufactured by Vuillaume studios around 1830-1832. The museum was so embarrassed that they took the first offer, who just happened to be Candi's dad. He had taken out a personal bank loan to purchase the violin and had it shipped to the musical conservator at the States Museum of Fine Arts. All of the museum's staff, with their Ph.Ds and Master's degrees swore it was a Stradivari. After cleaning and restringing, the violin was put on display for one year.

Even the bow was unique. The maker was Clement Eulry. One of the best French bow makers in the early 1800s. Eulry was the first to use a metal thumb facing on the bow's frog. The use of white horse hair for strings distinguishes the highest of quality. The bow was probably made after 1830 because of the metal facing. When the violin was shipped to the Museum of Fine Arts, it was in the original case with the bow in its holder. Candi's dad did not pay for the case or the bow, but was apparently part of the arrangement. This is why the sound from Candi's violin was all encompassing and projecting the sound in different dimensions. A Vuillaume is the second-best violin after a Stradivari.

Candi admitted her addiction to this violin. She would die if it was taken away. She was hooked on it. In our world, there are habits like drugs, alcohol, smoking and food or sex, gambling, shopping and a host of others. When it comes down to it, as human beings, we all have our own types of addiction.

This article was picked up by the county's independent journal and then a national newspaper. Life Magazine interviewed her and published it as a featured article; she did not bring her violin to the interview. One of her statements really hit home when she said, "We should be fighting a war on drugs, not killing people in other countries." Candi could sense things the majority of us cannot.

A great deal of the anonymous notes were written by females. They expressed concern about being coerced to try drugs and to be accepted as "cool." Others alarmingly described events where they were sexually attacked while being "high" or "stoned" but couldn't tell anyone about it because of the illegal activities that they were participating in. This sent Candi into a new crusade. She started the

Women's Union. Her first meeting was a packed house. Although the Women's Union was not limited to just female members, all students, teachers, staff and anyone else who felt compelled to contribute constructive criticism. The next meeting had to be held in the school's auditorium. The mayor and all members of the city council attended. She started a movement that is still in session today.

As the year winded down, Candi became a celebrity and was a guest speaker at the graduation ceremonies. The second graduating class stepped up on to the stage, with caps and gowns, accepting their diplomas. With dignity or being just plain silly. So, with that the class of 69 walked off the stage and into an unknown future.

The transferring of the cheating paperwork in the decoy locker had been working quite well for months. To accommodate the locker next to mine in one day, reinforced my suspicion that one or more coaches were helping Brad in his extortion plot against me. Just as long as they left Candi alone, I would keep up with the blackmail and put up with the insults and shoulder bumps, the elbows to the ribs and all the other displays of arrogance and superiority that I had to endure on a daily basis.

Copied from spiral notebooks

Chapter 11

But now the summer has arrived. Summer vacation started warm and full of hope. Right off the bat, I got a letter from Bob. He got the job and with his knowledge and construction experience, he was promoted to foreman. He managed a crew building concrete forms for the runways and foundations. The union was representing all workers so Bob joined. He was making more money than he ever had. The union has an apprenticeship program where he'd become a state certified carpenter. With his health insurance plan, the baby got medical attention whenever needed. They were happy and had found a home. He had had three other job offers since he got there. And he said that he owed it all to me for the work and help with the car and all the love that they'd never forget. He and the family might get some time off and come to see us this summer. Everyone can't wait to see the baby.

I saw this young kid pushing an old, beat up lawnmower around the neighborhood trying to drum up some business. I called him over and asked how much he charged for each job. After telling me, I said that wasn't enough. I asked if he wanted to work for me. I told him that he'd make money if he worked hard and cared about what he was doing. Also, I paid in cash. He was ready right then but I shook my head and said, "First we have to clean and maintain your mower." The kid's mower was shot. I rolled out my best mower, filled the tank, then we walked to old Hank's front lawn. I then pointed at three other front yards. "Get to work," I said. I also showed him how to use the edger and the wire rake.

At lunch, I brought him in the house and we had ham sandwiches with freshly-baked bread and big slices of ham on the bone with mustard and pickles. We ate a whole bag of granny goose potato chips with cokes to wash it all down. You should have seen the kid's face when I counted out his pay. I said that I'd work on his mower for him and show him how to maintain the mower each day. The kid was so happy. "What's your name again?" I asked.

"I'm Ronny, my real name is Ronald but I don't like it. So just call me Ronny."

"Where do you live, Ronny?"

"Oh, I live past 13th," he said shyly. That's the poor side of town.

"Here, I'll give you a note to give to your mom. It's got my name, address, and phone number on it. You tell her about the hard work you did today. And I want your mom to know the good work you're doing. So that's kind of a long way to walk home, don't you have a bike?"

"Yeah, I did, till it got run over in the driveway." He was probably working to buy another one.

"Well, tell you what, you can ride mine for a few days, OK?" Ronny was so happy as he rode away.

Early the next morning, an old Dodge Power Wagon pick-up truck pulled up to the house. Ronny got out and struggled to get my bike out of the back bed. I could hear the old high compression engine running roughly. I had to see this truck. Ronny had gotten the bike out and walked it to me. The truck backfired and shut down. From the driver's side door, Ronny's mom stepped out. Her afro was amazing. I was dressed as I always do when I'm working in the shop. Old grease-stained coveralls with a rag hanging out of my back pocket. A ruined baseball cap with a pair of cutting torch goggles above the brim. And the steel-toed boots. I must have looked terrible.

"Did you give Ronny that money and the bike?" she said sternly, arms akimbo while looking me up and down.

"Well," I said, "he earned every penny of it working."

"And what exactly did he do?" Hands still on her hips.

I pointed across the road at old Hank's front lawn. Perfectly cut, razor sharp edged and raked clean. Then I pointed further down the road. "He did all of those too." She was following my finger and then back to the first one.

"He did all that?" Her eyes wide with surprise.

"Yes, ma'am, and I just loaned him my bike."

Her eyes narrowed and she said, "How old are you?"

I couldn't help but smile. "My mom says I'm fifteen going on fifty." At that she laughed, relaxing a bit. "Is that your truck?" I asked as I walked up to it.

"It was my husband's. He was killed in the war. They said he was one of the Magnificent Bastards. They sent me his medal," she said, sounding very bitter. That really hurt me right in my heart.

"I am truly sorry, ma'am." She said nothing. "When you first pulled up, I could hear that the engine was running out of time. Can I have a look at it?"

"You know about things like that?" she asked, again looking me up and down.

"I rebuilt engines in my shop," I said pointing at the shop behind her. Then my mom and the Gomez sisters came out to the back porch.

"Miles, are you and your friends coming in for breakfast?" I looked back at Ronny and his mom.

"You'll eat like a king or I mean a queen." So, we all ate like royalty.

Pearl, Ronny's mom, could not believe the amount of food and activities around the table. Already on the table were ham and sausage. Fresh bread and a Dutch baby, scrambled eggs with salsa. Fried tomatoes, cottage fries and silver dollar pancakes. Milk and orange juice and strong coffee. The Gomez sisters were piling all of the serving plates and bowls on the table and pouring milk or coffee.

Old Hank sat at the head of the table. He had not cooked his breakfast for himself in many months. Ever since Candi and Hank's concert last summer, he had been a fixture in this house. I am usually awake in the wee hours of the morning, so I've heard and seen old Hank quietly leave his house and limps up the block and enter Gomez's sister's house. He is usually carrying his guitar.

With a cup of coffee in hand, I stood up and excused myself and Ronny from the breakfast table. Then, thanking the ladies of the house for an incredible meal. Old Hank held up his hand, stopping both of us. Hank looked right at Ronny and said, "You worked very hard yesterday and did a thorough job at my home. I talked to all the other neighbors and they would appreciate it if you would help them too."

Ronny was so surprised and happy that he blurted out, "Yes, sir."

"You can call me old Hank, deal?" Hank said this while holding out his wrinkled and leathered hand.

"Deal!" Ronny shouted out while shaking old Hank's hand.

As we were getting all the tools, I told Ronny that my dad was killed too. I said to him that being mad and upset would not help. To remember your dad and to be the best that you can, will make him proud and honorable. Learning, working and helping people is the best way to honor your dad.

Hours later, Pearl walked down the back stairs and over to the shop. I had pulled her truck onto the gravel driveway and had all the spark plugs and wires removed. I also had the distributor removed and was cleaning it.

She looked around at the scattered engine parts and said, "Now, how am I supposed to get home?"

"Well, it's going to take me a couple of days before I get this engine started," I said jokingly. "I'll work on your truck and you can drive Mom's car for a few days."

"So what will your mom drive?" she said.

I unconsciously let the truth come out of my mouth, "My mom hasn't driven her car for two years, she hasn't been out of the house in a long time. I don't think she'll mind, the tank's full and the car runs great."

Pearl wanted to talk to mom about the car. Pearl and Mom came down the backstairs laughing and carrying on. They both were carrying bags of leftovers and loading them into Mom's car. Then turning to me they walked up, Pearl smiling and shaking her head. "You win, Miles, and thank you, both of you, so very much for helping Ronny and me.

I'll be here tomorrow morning and we'll go out shopping, OK?" She gave me a hug and then hugged mom and left.

"Shopping?" I said curiously.

"Pearl and I are going to the store and shop for clothes, shoes, and stuff. I don't have a problem getting out of the house, Miles." She playfully poked me in the ribs, smiling while saying this. The next morning, Mom told Pearl that she was not feeling well but asked if Pearl could pick up some things for her. Mom had written a list.

I helped Ronny with trimming the hedges and cutting some lower tree limb. All the lawn clippings, hedge trimmings, and limb cutting I piled up in my backyard and burned in the late fall. Before I started the first pile of the season, Ronny and I dug up the soil with all the compost and ash from last year's burn and piled it by the side of the shop. This was enriched soil that I used in the planting beds of the clients around the neighborhood.

As we worked, I talked to Ronny about school and learning. I told him about my system of studying, and asked him if he would like to see how my system worked. I peaked his interest when I started talking about dinosaurs. He shyly admitted that his grades weren't so great.

Later that afternoon, I showed him my room. As you entered my room, the door didn't open all the way because of the bed. With the bed shoved against the far wall, it opened up the whole room. Normally the bed would be placed at the center of the huge window. The way the room is shaped, my desk was against the corner of the wall and window so that when I was sitting in my bankers office chair, I could easily see out the window. Walking into my room was like walking into a museum. The walls were all lined with shelves. My drafting table was opposite the desk so I could push away from the deck in my office chair and turn around and be at the drafting table.

The shelves were packed with rocks, dinosaur figures, books, and watercolor paintings of dinosaurs in their worlds along with auto parts. The closet was at the foot of the bed. All my clothes and shoes were organized, neat, and tidy. The rest of my room was boxes stacked on boxes, stacked on boxes. The room had a trail from the door to the closet, turn left and take two steps to the window. The desk was to the right, the drafting table to the left. It was the biggest bedroom in the house, but Mom didn't want it because she was reminded of Dad. My sister didn't want it because of the big window and being seen from the street. Ronny was amazed by the dinosaur paintings and figures. I told him that we could take a few hours a day to work on reading and writing. And work on outlines. In the meantime, I gave him several dinosaur books to read, then asked him to write down what he had learned from the books.

The weeks went by and the work kept coming in. Candi had gone to a summer music school for virtuosos. Not only were they teaching her the nuances of playing the violin, but also music history, reading and writing sheet music, and mathematics. She was also learning the piano.

Pearl had become a new member of the women's morning club. Since she worked part-time at a grocery store, she did all of the shopping for Mom. Pearl made pinto beans with ham hock and cornbread. It was delicious. She prepared several ethnic dishes and taught Mom and the Gomez sisters how to cook, what she called, poor folk's food. It didn't taste poor to me. I bought Pearl's husband's truck from her, then turned around and sold her a 1960 Volkswagen Beetle. I was given the car for free with the registration but only if I dragged the "bug" out of the garage that day. After rebuilding the motor and transaxle, replacing the wiring and new seat covers, the car looked brand new. Pearl loved it because the car was so easy to drive. She also gave me a kiss on my cheek for helping her son with his studies.

How could I not love such beautiful people? Pearl found a kindred affinity with my sister. They would take walks together and sit at the old picnic table under the pecan tree in the backyard. Always in deep and emotional conversation. Sometimes they were extremely serious, then erupted in loud laughter, and later quiet weeping. Pearl took my sister shopping for Mom and the Gomez sisters. Actually, it became a second job for Pearl because she would buy for old Hank too. They all insisted on paying Pearl for the work of shopping and delivery. She helped old Hank put away the groceries and household products. Then being very understanding and gracious, Pearl agreed to clean and maintain the kitchen and dining room weekly for Old Hank.

Later, Pearl told me a very confusing and strange thing. She told me that the first time she cleaned Old Hank's kitchen, he paid her one hundred dollars. The bill was flat, crisp like off the stack, brand new. She refused to take it, saying it was too much money. Old Hank, holding out the bill towards her, and with tears streaming down his cheek he said, "Please forgive me and help me pay for my past racist sins." Old Hank paid her the exact amount with the same type of currency every week. Pearl even urged my sister to fill out an application for part-time work at the grocery store.

After a month or so, my sister went out to a dance with her old high school girlfriends, and to a birthday party a week later. Pearl obtained all the paperwork for my sister to study and take the state's G.E.D. test. I just can't believe the wisdom, strength, and tenacity of this petite young woman. Ronny was also working very hard. Taking on tough jobs and not stopping till they were done. They easily became family and part of Saturday night dinners.

Candi came home during the last month of summer vacation. When she first saw me, she jumped in my arms. I hadn't seen her in just a few months, but Candi looked so different. She had filled out and had a beautiful bounce. Candi was so animated about all she had experienced at the music school. Her dad was now looking for a piano for sale. Candi instantly gravitated to Pearl and Ronny. We threw a grand welcome home party and a concert that Saturday night. Like a river, time always continues downstream.

Copied from spiral notebooks

Chapter 12

A week before school was to start, my sister did not come downstairs for breakfast. After a while, Mom went upstairs to wake her. No answer at her door. She was not in her room. It was too early for her to go on a walk, and usually she waited for Pearl. Breakfast was in full swing, but I still drove around the neighborhood. Candi had not seen her, and no one at the grocery store had seen her either. By the time I got home, Pearl was there waiting for me. Pearl intercepted me before I could get in the house. She was fearful for the whole family. Pearl had been trying to help my sister release her anxiety toward her baby. My sister perceived the demise of her fetus was tantamount to murder. Her approval of the voluntary termination of the child affected her state of mind and the fear of the future. In her nightly dream, she saw the blood on her hands as she held her dead baby.

Pearl grabbed my hand and said, "Oh Miles, I think your sister could have hurt herself."

I couldn't let Mom know how Pearl was feeling. Old Hank took over the driving search for my sister while I tried to find the phone numbers of my sister's old high school girlfriends. At first, the Gomez sisters didn't understand what was happening, but upon realizing the gravity of the situation, they sheltered Mom. By that time Candi had joined our plight.

Everyone echoed the same advice, call the police. Which is what Mom did. All that did was make things worse. The desk sergeant made it absolutely clear that the missing person was over eighteen years of age. There is a grace period of seventy-two hours before a missing person report can be filed for an adult. That time started when the person was first unaccounted for. So, in three days we could file a missing person report, and at that time the police would circulate a flier and picture with all the patrol officers to be on the lookout for my sister. They call it a B.O.L.O. Even when the authorities allowed us to file a missing person report, they were not proposing a dragnet county wide to locate my sister. If she was seen by a patrolman, they would question her and file a report. My mother was weeping and uttering unintelligible sentences, the telephone drooping in her hand. The Gomez sisters flanking my mom guided her away, while I took the phone. I let the officer know that we would continue the search and will be at his desk in three days to file the report. Candi and her father were staring at me intensely.

"Is she under a doctor's care?" Candi's dad questioned.

Yes, she was, maybe the doctor could persuade the police to act. The Gomez sisters said they knew the doctor and would speak to him for Mom. I couldn't find my sister's girlfriends' phone numbers but sort of knew where they lived. Old Hank was already out looking for my sister. Candi and her dad went downtown while I looked for my sister's girlfriends. Pearl was going to walk the same route that she and my sister had walked in the past. I got lucky when I saw the four-door sedan my sister's girlfriend picked her up in. After locating the correct front door, I was rewarded with my sister's girlfriend standing right in front of me. She had not seen her in two weeks. The last time she had seen my sister was at the birthday party two weeks ago. She seemed confused and worried when I told her that my sister was missing. She said that at the party there was a couple of boys smoking pot outside. She felt that those boys scared my sister and she was hiding from them. I asked her for the names of the pot-smoking boys but she didn't know them. I asked her to help us find my sister and tell the police about the boys at the party. She yelled, "No way!" and slammed the door in my face. She must have been afraid, but I would still give the police the information she had. She could also inform the police of the names of the other people who were at the party. These other people might know the boys' names. I stopped at a gas station and called home to see if there was any news about my sister.

Annie answered and told me to come home. Mom was having trouble breathing and standing up. When I returned, Mom was laying down on the couch. Fannie had called the doctor about my sister. Mom had briefly spoken to the doctor. The doctor wanted to see Mom and to come in for a medical appointment. Mom refused and hung up on him. My mom went into a panic and couldn't catch her breath. The Gomez sisters calmed Mom down and she was resting on the couch. Fannie called the doctor back and asked him to please talk to the police about my sister's mental state. It took all of us to get Mom in her bed. She was crying and moaning, calling out Dad's name to help her. On her nightstand was a picture of my sister's senior picture. I took it to a Fotomat and had one hundred copies made on full sheets of paper. The picture took up one-third of the paper and I wrote, "Have you seen me?" on the blank portion of the paper with our phone number on the bottom.

I had finished about thirty fliers when Candi and her dad returned without any sighting. They thought my idea was great and took several of the fliers to hang around downtown. I got a stapler and some masking tape out of the shop for them to use. We were standing outside when I told them about my sister's girlfriend's accounts and comments concerning the birthday party two weeks ago. I didn't want my mom to hear about this until she was stronger.

Pearl and Ronny came walking up to us from up the block. She was shaking her head side to side answering me before I could even ask. Candi handed Pearl one of the fliers and Pearl smiled at the picture of the beautiful young girl that is my sister. Candi and her father left to hang fliers, we all had a group hug before they went. Pearl, Ronny, and I went inside to finish the rest of the fliers. It was getting dark outside so there wasn't much else we could do. The Gomez sisters had warm food on the stove. They had cared for Mom all day, cleaned and straightened up the living room, and cooked an incredible dinner. I tried to thank them for all the kindness, compassion, and love that they had so generously given to my family, but I only got so far before I started choking up and then weeping. Fannie motherly pulled me to her ample bosom and held me as I cried. Pearl held her son's hand, got down on her knees, and hugged the boy tight, quietly shedding her tears. Ronny laid his head on his mom's shoulder and whimpered. Annie sat on the couch, sobbed into her handkerchief, shoulders heaving with every intake of breath. It was truly the beginning of the end for me.

When I woke up the following morning, I realized that I had slept for over seven peaceful and continuous hours. I felt invigorated and energized. I quickly got dressed and first checked on my mom who was still sleeping. Then to my sister's room which was empty. Downstairs, all was quiet. I set the water to boil and filled the percolator's sieve with coffee. The aroma reminded me of bygone mornings when my father would make coffee in this very coffee pot. Toasting day-old bread and covering it with clotted cream and strawberry jam. Sitting at the table we ate, drank and watched the sun rise. My dad would say that this is what human beings have done for thousands of years. They witness the birth of a new day. And that is exactly what I did.

The telephone rang loudly, just as the sun's whole body filled the sky. I had to squint my eyes to be able to see the phone. It was the police. They were willing to allow a missing person report to be filed because of the doctor's concern with my sister's mental state. I thanked them and arranged an eight o'clock interview for us that morning. Again, I thanked them and hung up.

I heard a soft moan and looked up to see Mom standing at the top of the stairs, gripping the top railing with both hands. Her face was drawn and the eyes had a wild look about them. My mom was realizing that she had to leave the house.

"You can do this, Mom," I said.

"I'll need help," she mumbled.

I called the Gomez sisters, thanking them profusely for all they had done. The only obstacle they foresaw was that they only had two hours to get my mom ready. An hour and a half later, I pulled my mom's car to the front of the house. Freshly cleaned and vacuumed, washed and buffed to a glimmer. The 64 Chevelle SS purred like a tiger. I have invested a great deal of time and money into this car, hoping to entice my mom into getting out of the house. Old Hank saw me and limped across the street to ask about my sister and Mom. I told him everything, the birthday party, the fliers, and this morning's trip to the police station. That made him feel a little better. But he vowed that whoever had any part in my sister's disappearance, will pay dearly.

I did something I never thought I would. I hugged Old Hank and kissed him on the cheek and softly said, "Thank you," in his ear. That grizzled old man hugged me back then turned and limped away, suppressing his tears. I had no idea that this would be the last time I would see this great man.

I heard the front door open and the ladies stepping out. I knew not to overreact to my mom's descending the front porch stairs. She looked stunning. I was astonished. A very conservative knee-length dress, her long blonde hair curled and bouncy. Her makeup is perfect but, like her smile, subtle and dignified. Her figure was still trim and muscular which enhanced the fact that she was well-endowed. The Gomez sisters as always were prim and proper. Everyone was ready to go. Mom and I in the front and the Gomez sisters in the back. I could see my mom's hands shaking.

First we went to the doctor's office to receive a letter from the doctor describing my sister's medical conditions. The ladies did not want to go in so I went in alone. Dr.

Bridgewater personally came out into the waiting room to present the letter to my mom and was disappointed when he realized that she was not there. He was adamant about my mom making an appointment to see him soon. I reassured him that I would tell my mom and thanked him for all of his help and concern.

From there, we traveled directly to the City Police Station. I parked in the parking lot provided for the public. The newly built Police Station is used by the county and city, which is why it is now called Unified Police Station. Its construction is steel, concrete and tinted glass. It is very futuristic. I opened the glass doors at the main entrance of the police station for the ladies and found everyone a place to sit. The shaking of my mom's hands was more pronounced. I put my hands on hers and smiled, hoping to stop her agitation. There were several people sitting in various areas around a very large and tall reception desk. I straightened my tie as I went to the reception desk and spoke to a young woman with startling, beautiful, light blue eyes. I tripped over my tongue and tried again to introduce myself and to mention my scheduled appointment. The receptionist's beauty had truly enchanted me and that had caught me off guard. I recently seemed to be more interested in the female form than ever before. She asked me to wait one moment and picked up a ringing phone with multiple push-buttons. Not wanting to stare, I turned to see how Mom was coping with being out of the house. The ladies were chatting calmly. The receptionist called my name and I swiftly turned back to face the desk, knocking over a tray of administration pamphlets. The majority of them fell onto her lap.

"If you're trying to ask me out for a date, you're doing a pretty good job," she said, smiling and with a little laugh. I could feel the heat from my face. She stood and said, "Follow me." The ladies were already standing and walking forward. Upon seeing this, the receptionist explained, "Only family members are allowed in, I am truly sorry." The last part she directed to me putting her hand gently on my arm. Her hand felt warm and soft.

The Gomez sisters instantly said, "We understand." This was Fannie. "We'll wait right here." That was Annie. They turned and walked back to their seats as we went down a very long hallway. This blue-eyed beauty took us to a door with numbers on it, opened it and said, "First desk on your right." I thanked her and let my mother enter first. Just as my mom stepped in, the blue-eyed beauty winked at me. I smiled back and thanked her with the deepest voice I could muster.

In the room were six desks in all manner of disarray. A sink and countertop with a coffee machine on it was perched in the far right corner of the room. A uniformed officer with three stripes on the side of his shoulder was making a cup of coffee. There was no one else in the room. He turned toward us and walked to the first desk on the right. He did not offer us any coffee.

"Have a seat," he said while loudly slurping his coffee. We sat in uncomfortable institutional metal chairs with very little padding. We couldn't sit up close because of the full straight back metal desk. "We have a very long process to fill out a missing person report, so let's get started."

I anticipated this so I handed over all the information I had compiled. Also, I brought documents from school, a birth certificate, and of course the letter from the doctor. I had also included a written affidavit of my interview with my sister's girlfriend. I found her name in an old yearbook along with the other girlfriend who also went to the party with my sister. Someone had to know who the boys at the party were. The desk sergeant looked at the first couple of pages and started transferring information onto the missing person report. After a while, the sergeant asked a simple question, "What is this?" then sat back in his comfortable reclining office chair looking at the affidavit.

"That is information about my sister's disappearances that should be investigated." I made it plain and simple.

The desk sergeant stared at me for a minute then said, "I checked on your sister's record, arrested for being a minor in possession of alcohol, drunk in public and lewd acts in public. Charges dropped. She also was suspended from school several times and finally expelled. Now the doctor's letter states that your sister has run away from home twice. Now, the way I see it, your sister has caused a lot of trouble for us, so she's an adult now and we ain't babysitting her no more. I'll put out a BOLO on her tomorrow at the morning's shift change. If I hear anything, I'll call ya." With that, he put the affidavit down in front of me and gathered up the other papers signifying the interview was over. My mom's lips were trembling. Not with the presence of tears, but in an act of furious rage.

To defuse an imminent conflict, I stood and said, "I need the original birth certificate and doctor's letter back, you can make xerox for your file."

"No," he said while stacking the paperwork into a manila envelope.

My mother stood up slowly. I turned toward her, my arms coming up. And that is when Detective Hansen opened the door and walked in. The desk sergeant sat up straight.

"Good morning, Miles," Detective Hansen said, walking toward me and shaking my hand. "And this must be your mother." Detective Hansen ignored the sergeant. I introduced him to my mom, and explained the need for the documents to be copied. Only then did Detective Hansen acknowledge the sergeant, "Is that going to be a problem, sergeant?"

"No, sir." The desk sergeant quickly jumped up to go when the Detective stopped him.

"On the other hand, make two copies of the whole file, one for your department, one for me, and all of the original paperwork given back."

"Yes, sir." The sergeant walked out, flashing a glance at me as he went. Detective Hansen reassured my mom that he'd do everything he could to locate my sister. He was very impressed with my fliers and asked if he could keep one. Detective Hansen told us that he knew my father, that he admired and respected my father. He owed my father a great deal. When he heard that we were here, he came down to help in any way. Before I could stop her, Mom told Detective Hansen that the desk sergeant was extremely rude. He knew that was another reason why he came down to help. He then reassured us that we will not have any more problems. The sergeant returned and politely gave us our original file back. Detective Hansen walked us back to the main reception area and gave Mom one of his business cards and introduced himself to the Gomez sisters. I noticed that my mom's hands were not shaking. During all of that, the woman with the beautiful light-blue eyes, waved me over and handed me a slip of paper.

"You'll need this," and quickly answered a ringing phone.

As I walked back to my party, I unfolded the paper and found in exquisite cursive her name and phone number. I fumbled to get the reception's front glass doors open for the ladies. Stumbled while walking down the steps and dropped my car keys twice before we got to the car. What's wrong with me?

I got the ladies seated in the car. They were chatting about the tall, dark, and handsome Detective Hansen. I backed the car out of the parking place and drove out onto the street. Instantly, a city police squad car's red lights flashing motioned for me to pull over, which I did. From my rear-view mirror, I saw two police officers get out of the car and walk up to my side of the car. I rolled my window down just as the young police officer said, "License and registration please." While I handed him the registration, I explained that I had no state's driver license.

"Sir, it's illegal to drive a motor vehicle without a driver's license." I couldn't see the other officer to my right, he was standing up straight so all I could see was him from the chest down. What I could see were the three stripes on the side of his shoulder. "Please wait here." They walked back to the squad car. The ladies were troubled and uneasy. My mom was staring at me nervously. Her hands were shaking with pure fright. The officers returned to the same position as before. "Sir, I have written you a citation for driving without a license. I need you to get out of the driver's seat and sign the ticket please." After following the officer's orders, he asked if anyone in the car had a driver's license. Annie said she did and eventually fished it out of a huge handbag. "Ma'am, this license expired eleven years ago. I'm afraid I have to confiscate this license. You can apply for a new one." Since I had stepped out of the car, I had been staring into the eyes of the desk sergeant over the roof of the car. When the young officer handed me my copy of the ticket, the sergeant wrapped his knuckles on the passenger window startling my mom. He made a roll-the-window-down gesture to my mom. After she did, he asked her if this was her name on the registration. She was so frightened, all that came out of her mouth was a groan. "OK then, put your registration back in the glove box. And here's your citation for contributing to the delinquency of a minor."

"Well, I never!" shouted Fannie. "What is the meaning of this?"

"This is none of your business!" snarled the sergeant, thrusting the paper at Mom.

"You have to sign this," the sergeant said leaning further into the car. I slid into the car seat and hastily snatched the papers out of the sergeant's hand. He gave me a menacing look. I ignored him and helped my mom sign the ticket, then handed it to the young officer. He separated the two pieces of paper and handed me the carbon copy.

"OK everyone, let's get out of the car, we'll all go to the diner," I said cheerfully like we were all going on an outing. I already knew what was coming.

"You can pick up your car at the impound yard," the sergeant said snidely.

I turned to the young officer and asked, "What was your probable cause for pulling me over?"

He was quite surprised by my question but the desk sergeant shouted out, "Failure to use your turn signal." I will deal with him later.

We walked across the street to a red and white diner and got settled in. I asked for water, coffee, and menus all around, thanking the waitress. From there, I went to the bathroom, washed my hands, straightened my tie in the mirror. Looking at my reflection in the mirror, I considered my options. What did the blue-eyed woman see in me? Why did the desk sergeant resent me? Why did my sister run away, and that's what I think she did, she's running away from herself. The desk sergeant certainly has a grudge against my father. And the blue-eyed beautiful wants to have sex with me because she sees me as who I am, a virgin. In the hallway leading to the bathroom was a pay phone and phone book. I found a taxi service and asked for a pick-up at the diner. At the table, they had waited for me before ordering. I suggested we just order some ice cream before our taxi arrived. Mom looked at me and smiled. I held her shaking hand and said, "You're doing great, Mom."

The Gomez sisters were furious the way the police treated us and wanted to complain to the superintendent. But I had another idea. Once we got home, I called Detective Hansen. The operator switched me to his department and a raspy voice explained that the Detective was out on a homicide call. I left a message. Then I called the City Impound Yard. They said that I had to wait till the car came in and was processed. Maybe tomorrow. So, I called Pearl and asked if she would give me a ride to the impound yard. I will answer all her questions tomorrow. She agreed but had to do it at her lunch break. I offered to pay her, buy gasoline, and take her out to lunch. She refused but gave in for lunch. She had hung all the fliers and been out all morning looking for my sister but had found nothing. I thanked her and said that I would walk to the grocery store, we could leave from there then. Mom said that she hadn't slept at all last night and was exhausted. She needed to sleep but she had to have a sleeping pill. The Gomez sisters dotted around Mom till she was tucked in under the covers.

I kissed my sleepy mother's forehead and said, "Everything is going to be alright." That's when I realized, my first recollection of my mom.

She was leaning over, kissed me on the forehead and said, "Everything is going to be OK."

When Mom closed her eyes, we went downstairs and started fixing lunch. I knew that Ronny was a freelancer, working up the street, so I called him over to have a light late lunch with us. The Gomez sisters could never prepare a light meal, so we ate like kings and I had leftovers for dinner. I laid down onto my bed at nine o'clock at night. I closed my eyes. The image I saw was of the desk sergeant, sneering at me over the roof of my mom's car. I wanted to kick his teeth down his throat that very second. When he went to make copies of my file, he probably looked up our police records.

He saw that my mom's driver's license was expired and I didn't have one. So, he grabbed a rookie cop and waited for us to drive out. Pulled us over for any slight infraction and humiliated us. Just because the detective put him in his place or because my father did the same thing, long ago.

Whatever! I decided I was going to make his life very uncomfortable. Floating up from the soup of hate, I see the light blue-eyed beauty. Her long and straight nut-brown hair curling at the ends. The pixie nose and perfect jawline. With the slightest degree of downturn of her eyelids in the lower outside corners of her eyes. Her slender body as she sashayed down the hallway. My erection embarrassed me.

Softly and slowly, my eyelids opened, just in time to see the sun creep up my window sill. I slept all night. My digital flip clock said it was 5:58, I got up and put on my robe. There was a large lump under the covers on my mom's bed, and it's snoring. Checked! I jumped in the shower and returned to my room. It dawned on me that I hadn't checked on my sister's room. The Gomez sisters were not here yet, they had a key for the front door. They usually used the kitchen door every morning. It's never locked, usually. With my coffee cup in hand, I entered my shop.

Surveying the contents, I see my neglect. It'd been several days since anything had been worked on. I was in the middle of three engine jobs that had to be finished. And the 454 was a bitch. What could I get done in three hours? At the end of that three hours, I had the small block done. The straight six was ready to be torqued. And the 454 was still a bitch.

The Gomez sisters yelled at me three times that breakfast was ready, come and get it! Earlier I sent Candi back to eat breakfast, after she brought me a cup of coffee. I entered the house from the back porch door directly into the kitchen. Our kitchen is a very big space. The original Wedgewood stove remains but the more modern stove fits right next to it. The Gomez sisters bought it and had it installed for better cooking convenience. They shared the one exhaust vent. The far wall is all windows and the back porch door. In the far corner, with a view of the back yard, is a small breakfast table where my mom was sitting. She was wearing her old but comfortable house coat. Her hair was pulled back into a single ponytail. The coffee in front of her was stone cold. Her affixed gaze was centered on the pecan tree where for years she and my sister felt safe and sheltered. I kissed her forehead and whispered in her ear, "She will come back, Mom, we're going to get her back."

The Gomez sisters frowned at me for missing breakfast. I shrugged my shoulders "Sorry." Then I grabbed a large piece of ham, folded it like a taco, and filled it with fried potatoes. Eating it as I ran upstairs to clean up.

In the bathroom, taking the last bite, I noticed that my hands were greasy and I had been eating it. Oh well! Eat the last bite grease and all. Showered, brushed my teeth and hair and headed out the bathroom with a towel wrapped around me trotting to my bedroom. Dressed and ready to go, I paused at my desk for some paperwork. When the sergeant was handing my mom the citation to be signed, I had palmed the registration out of the glove box. I had my ticket, Mom's ticket, and the car registration laid out on my desk. I knew the sergeant would impound the car if no licensed driver were present. I bought used auto parts from impound cars that weren't released to the owner for a number of reasons. I knew where the impound yard was because it's where all the auto junkyards store their inventory. There are other departments and county properties. This is where the dog pound, the dumps, and the sewer treatment plant are. All of these county district organized systems, and business enterprises are located just before the huge old railroad yard, and the Red river. I wrote a short letter and counted out three hundred dollars from my cash stash. The money, the tickets, and registration, I placed in my briefcase. Downstairs I found my mom sitting on the couch. I showed her the letter and asked her to sign it. I told her my plan. I'll bring the car home. We'll speak to Detective Hansen about the tickets and the sergeant's behavior. Then I'll look for my sister until we get her back. Tears were streaming down her cheeks, hesitating there for a few moments then plunging on to her housecoat. Her housecoat glistened with her tears. She signed the letter. I kissed her forehead then quickly left before I broke down.

The walk to the grocery store helped me to shed some of my doubts about my sister. She did run away before. And she was an adult with the right to whatever life she chose. I waved at Pearl when I entered the store and bought two apples from the produce. I was leaning on her car as Pearl walked up to me and caught the apple I threw to her.

"What's this?" she inquired.

"Lunch," I explained. "Let's go."

A Volkswagen Beetle is a fun car to drive but a terrible place to hold a conversation. It took a lot of "whats" and "say that again" before Pearl understood everything. Pearl had a current driver's license so she could legally purchase custody of the vehicle by paying for the tow, storage, and any fines. The letter Mom signed granted permission for Pearl to pick up the car. The registration was the final document of proof. It was a bit of a drive and toward the end, the road got narrow and bumpy.

When we drove through the impound's big double gates, we knew I would have to drive the Beetle through the impound's gates going out. With no license, I did not want anyone to see me. We would have to do it again after going out. I stayed in the car and let Pearl take care of all financial expenditures with the three hundred dollars I gave her along with the other paperwork. We had parked further down the lot so that no one at the impound yard could see me drive away. I have no license.

Something was wrong. Pearl was talking adamantly with the person inside the service window. She turned and walked back toward me. Shaking her head "no," she opened the door saying that the car wasn't there. It had to be here! I had to double check. The impound yard had provided for the public a bank of new payphones in a row with individual phone books. They were outside against the wall of the impound's office, each with their own small roof and little table. I called the Unified Police Station, and was put on hold, was transferred twice then hung-up on. I called back and to my surprise the voice of the blue-eyed beauty filled my ear. She instantly recognized my voice and after I sincerely divulged my plight to her, she became very serious. She had me write down a phone number, then asked me for the number I was calling from. She said the number she gave me was her phone number at her station. She said that she would find the tow service that picked up my car and would call back to the number I gave her. I told her that I could not thank her enough for her help. She said, "Yes, you can," and hung up.

Oh my, I was starting to feel embarrassed again. Pearl used another phone to ask work if she could take an hour more off to help a friend. Then called my house to ask the Gomez sisters if they would feed Ronny lunch. They both laughed at the same time saying that he was already here, and not to worry. I had told Candi everything about the police interview, the sergeant, and the car at the impound yard this morning in my shop. She was upset that anyone would be so disrespectful toward my mom. I had never seen her that mad before. Candi wanted to come back over later to stay with my mom for a while. Pearl said Candi was there now. That made me feel good knowing she was there. The phone rang in my impromptu payphone office. The blue-eyed beauty told me that a tow service called Provider Wreckers and Outfitters were the contractors to the city for tow service. She could not find any ticket copies or dockets to impound my mom's car yesterday. She had the contractor's address. 32 Salvage Road, off of Industrial Way. The impound yard was on Industrial Way and Salvage Road, where the various auto junkyards I buy from, were located. The blue-eyed beauty told me that I had both her numbers and said, "Call me."

I've been in this area many times. Salvage Road is a straight line of fenced-in junked cars stacked on top of each other by the thousands. We drove past the auto salvage yards I had done business with in the past. I hadn't gone any further up the road than that. The Bug bumped and bounced its way up the road for a few more minutes until I slammed on the brakes. In front of the Bug was a huge gate with a metal sign above it announcing, "Provider Wreckers and Outfitters," tow trucks, heavy equipment, and cranes. A little river of oil, hydraulic, and transmission fluid and probably eleven other toxic chemicals was trickling out of the front gate. Just past and outside the gate, the reason I stopped so quickly, was my mom's car on cinder blocks. The engine and transmission, gone! The front wheels and suspension, gone! The rear wheels and rear axle, gone! The fenders, hood and trunk, gone! The interior, gone! The only thing that remained was the rear license plate, laying on the ground which I knew by heart. It had been stripped completely in less than twenty-four hours. I turned the Bug around and jumped out. I put Pearl in the driver's seat and told her to wait for me, but if anyone other than me came out the gate, split!

I couldn't even look at the car so I went straight in, passed hundreds of cars stacked on top of each other until I saw a boxcar with a front porch. One dog came out barking like a rabid animal and was running right for me. It was all teeth, fangs, and slobber. I ignored it completely. An older dog limping barked once or twice then gave up and laid down. The ferocious and crazy wild beast jumped up and down, back and forth, barking and snarling. Baring its teeth threateningly. I didn't give it any notion at all, just walked right up the steps onto the front porch.

It was a Cadillac rear bench seat bolted to a heavy metal frame. Upon which sat a man of tremendous girth. His stomach overlapped his legs just above his knees. A dirty head of hair with a beard to match. The red nose and beady-eyes recessed in the hair. I made no reaction to the cigarette butts, old food, and the stink. The dog had stopped barking and heeled by my leg. I nonchalantly petted him on his head.

"What you want, boy?" The voice was that of a destroyed throat, sounding like walking on gravel. Cigarette butts scattered everywhere.

"I'm sorry to bother you, sir, but could you tell me about the car outside your gate please," I said with a cheerful smile.

"Driver got to the yard late. Gate was locked. Had to leave it outside the gate. I already called the cops." Maybe the voice sounded more like dragging a dead body across the gravel.

"I need a police report for my insurance company, sir. Does this kind of thing happen a lot?" I said making light of it.

"My insurance says I have credible security, anything outside my gate ain't my responsibility," he said all of this while fishing out a cigarette from a crumpled pack and lighting it with a blowtorch.

"What did you say the name of the tow truck operator was again, sir?" I asked politely.

"I didn't," the fat man said, blowing out smoke. "I don't like you, boy, you're some sort of a smart-ass. I know who you are motherfucker, so if you fuck with me, I'll kill you and your whole family. And I know people who will do it too." That was it. I could have picked up any metal object laying around me and bashed his skull in – but.

"No, sir, I wouldn't do anything, I mean I'm sorry to have bothered you, sir. I just want my insurance money, sir. I'll never bother you again, sir," I said all of this backing up and cowering before him.

At the bottom of the steps, I turned and walked quickly past the canyons like rows of crushed vehicles, huge piles of engines, and acres upon acres of cranes, semi-trucks, and heavy equipment. As I exited the gate, I took notice of the big Yale padlock, and one more look at my mom's stripped car. I had put hundreds of dollars into that car. I had hoped it would encourage my mom to get out of the house and continue with her life. I feared that our lives had been intricately transformed. Snapping out of this trance, I realized exactly what I have to do.

I let Pearl drive. I took the money and the paperwork back from Pearl. Back on the county highway and just before the city limits, I asked Pearl to drop me off at the Esso filling station. She was extremely confused. I hadn't told her anything about the events inside the scrapyard. As I got out, I said to her, "I'm sorry I got you mixed up in this, and I understand that you will do what you think is right. Thank you so very much."

With that said, I closed the door and walked away without looking back. I used the payphone, remembering the number for the yellow cab I had called yesterday for a pick-up. From there, I went into the bathroom and violently vomited in the toilet. My plan sickened me.

The cab dropped me off at the county library which is two blocks away from the city police station. The brand-new library is dedicated to E.J. Underwood, a city founder and the financier of the first library. The dimension of this new library encompassed a block long and a block wide. The entrance was all glass and featured an art gallery with a bust of E.J. Underwood and a seating and conversation area. Beyond that were public restrooms and several payphones in the hallway. Using one of the payphones, I called the blue-eyed beauty. Since this city was the county seat, the city and county had joined forces and combined the brand-new buildings for all law enforcement agencies. She picked up after the first ring and spoke professionally but changed her tone when she realized it was me. After a few moments of pleasantries, I asked if Detective Hansen was there.

"Hold on," she said. A minute later, she was back on the line and asked when I could come in to meet with Detective Hansen. I told her ten minutes. As soon as I opened the front glass doors of the Unified Police Station, Detective Hansen was standing by the tall reception desk. The blue-eyed beauty ignored me completely. He ushered me in an elevator and pushed the lower level button. Not a word was spoken. Through the elevator doors I followed him into a tiny room that was very cold.

That's when he spoke, "I called your home about an hour ago. A woman named Candi said you would be back this afternoon. Thanks for coming down. I didn't want to talk to your mother."

"No problem, sir, what can I do to help?" I already knew.

The Detective removed one of my fliers from his briefcase, asking if that was my sister. I assured him that it was.

"Can you view a homicide victim for a possible identification?" he asked stone-faced.

"Yes." I knew.

He turned on a light switch and illuminated a space behind the glass panel in the far wall. A person wearing a hospital gown, cap, and mask looked directly at us. The medical personnel was a female. With gloved hands, she lifted the corners and pulled back the sheet, resting the folded portion on the chest. She then stepped back out of view. Now I knew why Detective Hansen referred to the flier. Whoever did this, was trying to make identification impossible. The mouth and nose were ruined. From the chin to just below the eyes, the destruction was complete. The face was caved in. With the nose and mouth crushed, the force collapsed the face into the skull's cavity. I bent my knees deeply to see just the profile of the face. This was my sister and she had been murdered. Like my mother, my sister was well-endowed. The sheet folded over my sister's chest gave way to gravity and slid down to her stomach. With her ample breasts exposed, also exposed was the deep knife wounds in her chest between her breasts. Detective Hansen tapped on the glass and the medical personnel moved swiftly to cover my sister completely.

Frowning, because of the distraction, Detective Hansen turned to me and asked, "Do you need more time?"

"She should have a birthmark on her right inside ankle," I said this with tears running down my face.

Detective Hansen handed me a handkerchief, flipped off the light switch then opened the door. All fluid movements with practiced precision.

"That mutilated body in there is my sister. I have identified her. My mother cannot see her like that." I pleaded.

So, Detective Hansen and I took the elevator to the fourth floor and I signed two affidavits, I was given copies. The detective told me that my sister's body would be here for two days for evidence collection. I would be told when my family could come and get her. We could have our choice of arranging a funeral home to service our needs, or the county's contracted mortician will be called to transport my sister when all was ready. Then the detective told me that a newspaper reporter heard about the murder at the old railroad yard on a police scanner.

"He was there and took pictures of the body. He tried to question me but I told him nothing. He had one of your fliers in his hand. I tried to stop him, I'm sorry."

There was something cold in Detective Hansen's eyes. His face was like granite, and his emotions nonexistent. I had to get to my mom. On the ground floor, I walked down the main hallway away from the reception area. At the end of the hallway were the doors to the police parking yard. I saw this yesterday. Out in the parking yard, I saw a pedestrian gate that allowed foot traffic out but not in. Back at the library, I phoned for another taxi and bought a newspaper.

It was the morning edition, nothing about the murder. I waited outside for the taxi. Finally coming through the front door, I stopped and took a breath. Candi was looking at me from the couch.

"The detective called for you," she said in a hushed voice. I pointed up and she nodded her head up and down. Mom's asleep. I pointed to the kitchen door. She put down her book and walked to the kitchen with me right behind. I said nothing and kept walking right out the kitchen door and to the shop. Candi followed me till I closed the shop door behind us.

I could not contain myself anymore and started weeping like a baby. Sobbing, I crumpled to the ground, Candi falling with me. I couldn't speak and I was gulping air. My body is going into convulsion. My eyes were slits pouring out tears, I was crying out and now screaming. I saw her, her face. The teeth and bones, white and broken. Her breast bruised with deep stab wounds between them. I was screaming, screaming, and I couldn't stop. Pounding the dirt floor with my hands, screaming till my throats shredded and bloody raw.

My mommy was there, holding me, her arms like wings shrouding me. Protecting me from my own self-destruction. Through my screams, I faintly heard my mommy humming a song from long ago. Exhausted from struggling with what was binding me, I gave up, my body went limp and I peed my pants. This was what Candi told me had happened.

The last thing I remembered was taking a deep breath by the front door. I found myself laying on the living room floor. My hands wrapped in gaze, my pants and underwear gone. A towel wrapped around my skinny waist. I was covered in dirt and oil. I was temporarily insane. I felt ashamed. I needed to be strong for my mom but failed miserably. I started crying again, I told Candi that my sister was dead. She said that everyone knew, it was all in the paper. Mom was upstairs sleeping, the Gomez sisters were with her. My failure was complete.

"What happened to my pants?"

Candi smiled and said, "Took them off and cleaned you. You have a beautiful body, Miles."

I was looking at her with my mouth half-opened, not knowing what to say. She leant forward and kissed me passionately. "Now, go get cleaned up," she said, pushing me away playfully. I told her to go home and do the same. After a shower, I put band-aids on the minor cuts on my hands. Nothing could be done about the bruise on my forehead. The Gomez sisters kissed and hugged me with puffy red eyes. They were sitting in Mom's bedroom while she slept. She probably saved my life when she soothed me from my insanity.

All was quiet in the house so I read the paper then the police files Detective Hansen had given me. All the paperwork was labeled "for department use only." The Detective didn't have to give this paperwork. I think Detective Hansen wanted me to know he cared. The files stated that all the injuries were postmortem. Death was probably an overdose of some sort of drug. Several recent injection sites were noted. Blood tests were pending.

The only thing I had eaten that day was a ham and potato taco and an apple. There were breakfast leftovers in the kitchen so I made a hodgepodge omelet and toast. I ate it in the shop while cleaning things up. I called the client who owned the short block engine to inform him that it was ready for pick-up. He'd be here by six. I had to do something or I'd lose it again. Finishing these engines but not taking on any more work helped me cope with this stress. I needed to think through the direction of my objectives, now even more. By the time I came back into the house, everyone was sleeping. I called Candi to say I love you and good night. I used the bathroom, then quietly walked to my bedroom. I sat at my desk to write a list and a timetable. I started a file with my sister's name on the tab. The paperwork from the detective, the tickets and registration for Mom's car went right in the file. The newspaper article I cut out and wrote the date on it then added it to the file. There were two fliers left over that Ronny used as examples for him to copy.

Copied from spiral notebooks

Chapter 13

My sister's image stared at me accusingly. I begged her to forgive me, but she would not. Not until she was avenged! Not until they all were dead. I was not given a choice. For a human to kill for amusement, revenge must be inhumane. I knew that the only way I could live with myself was to become my sister's avenger. My mind would now rest and I could go to sleep as a boy then wake as a man.

The false dawn was shimmering in my eyes, but that's not what had awoken me. It was the opening and closing of my bedroom door. I turned to see and squinted from the harsh sunlight. I could just see Candi taking off her bra and pulling down her panties.

"Move over, give me some room," she said in a very hushed voice. With her right hand, she grabbed my erection as her left hand held the condom which she unrolled down my cock. At the same time, she threw her right leg over me, straddling my hips. She guided me into her, pushing her pelvis down and accepting me inside her. She laid on my chest, her mouth close to my ear. A prolonged low moan escaped from her, the breath hot and with a subtle scent of peppermint. She raised her hips slowly, then brought them down even slower, repeating the movement and gradually increasing the repetition. I placed my hands on her hips and added a little pressure with her rhythm. She sat up just a bit and allowed me to fully penetrate her body. I could no longer hold back my lust and desire. My release took my breath away, and I arched my back until my body quivered and trembled. Candi suddenly stopped, she was now sitting straight up on me and we grasped each other's hands. Her head tilted back, eyes closed tight. Just a little gasp then her whole body shook just for a second, then again, and again. She let out a long-held breath and collapsed on top of me. Catching our breath, Candi said, "Let's do that again."

"Can you give me fifteen minutes, you just took my virginity," I joked. Candi rolled off of me and hurryingly got dressed. I lay there watching her. A toned, strong body. Broad hips and a narrow butt with dimples on each side. She was wearing an under-wire bra because her breasts were more than average size, full, upright, and muscular. With the most delicate and petite areolas and nipples. This was a strikingly beautiful and stunning woman. As she zipped up and snapped her pants, she looked up at me with a devilish smile.

Kneeling down by my bedside, she lovingly kissed me and said, "I needed that, and so did you. Give me five minutes in the bathroom, then you go and get yourself cleaned up and ready for breakfast. Then we need to do everything we can for your sister, OK."

My smile was her answer, so off she went. We do have to do that again.

In the kitchen, the activities were quiet and reverent. The Gomez sisters were alternating shifts to be by Mom's side at all times. I don't know how I do it but I can tell the difference between the Gomez sisters instantly and accurately. They try to trick me, but it never works. Annie asked me how I wanted my eggs, which was just the start of my huge breakfast. The topic of conversation was not about my sister but about my mom. She was suffering from debilitating migraine headaches. She had also experienced several nervous breakdowns. Also, my mother had a disease called agoraphobia. This is a social anxiety or a fear of leaving one's house. My mom had an intense fear of physically walking past the front door's threshold. But astonishingly, my mother endured a drive to the doctor's office parking lot. Then to the city police station. After which, we were pulled over and forced out of our vehicle. Seeking shelter in a roadside diner and then a cramped ride home in a smelly taxi.

My mom had returned very ill from her unnecessary appointments. My mom couldn't travel to the doctor's office. So, I called the doctor's office and asked to speak with Dr. Bridgewater about my mother's condition. The secretary assured us that Dr. Bridgewater would be there for the five o'clock house-call. The first thing I needed to do was talk to my mom. When I entered her bedroom, Fannie was softly crying while Mom held her hand comforting her. Fannie gave me a hug as she left. I told Mom about the house-call and questioned her about the migraines. Her descriptions of the headaches were horrifying. The skull-pounding pain. Vision lost. Days of intense, fluctuating pain like an ocean wave receding away from the shore then returning and crashing against the rocks with a violent explosive force. She told me about her uncontrollable fear that just beyond her front door was the evil, wicked, and despicable people, like that worthless sergeant, and the victims who will lash out against anyone who showed weakness or fragility. My mom's pain, fear, and anxiety made her sleep impossible.

The Gomez sisters cleaned Mom's bedroom, took out all of the laundry and changed all the bed linens. From there, they gave Mom a hand bath and helped her dress into her nightgown and robe. Candi and I cleaned the kitchen and living room. She kissed me on the cheek, and with a wink, said goodbye to go home and help her mom with the baby. She would come back tonight to see how the doctor's visit went.

Dr. Bridgewater was exactly on time. He went directly upstairs. During that time, my mother screamed out in an erotic release. When he was descending the stairs, he was writing in a small notebook. The doctor's medical advice was a new drug called Quaalude for my mom's agoraphobia. Then, for the nervous breakdowns he prescribed valium, taken when needed. Codeine prescription was for the unbearable pain from the migraines. And a higher-than-normal dose of Barbiturates for insomnia. I agreed to fill all the prescriptions first thing in the morning. Dr. Bridgewater sternly instructed the regimental treatments and the importance of these medications. I whole-heartedly agreed with him, then I handed the doctor a folded piece of paper and asked the doctor if he would sign this letter. After a few seconds of deliberation, the doctor looked up at me and said, "But of course." Out of thin air, I magically produced a pen with blue ink and presented it to the doctor. He signed it and handed the letter back to me, but he pocketed the pen. Before he left, he expressed his sympathy and condolences for the loss of my sister. We offered him coffee and something to eat but the doctor declined pleading for appointment punctuality and left abruptly. Mom was sleeping soundly so the Gomez sisters said their good nights, going out the kitchen door and walking home. Candi was frustrated but said she had to go home.

"In four days, we start our junior year of high school, Miles, I've got to get ready!" With that, she kissed me and out the kitchen door she went. I leant on the old Wedgewood stove with six burners and dual ovens. The pilot lights kept the porcelain-coated iron frame warm. Eating the finger food and drinking the coffee that was intended for the doctor's consumption. In the low light warmth, I pondered my destructive engineering.

The phone rang annoyingly. I didn't want the ringing to wake my mom so I answered the phone swiftly. It was Detective Hansen. He did not beat around the brush, he got right to the point.

"Do you know Henry Louis Stein?"

"No, I don't know anyone with that name."

"Well, his identification shows that he lives on your block."

"What? Do you mean Old Hank?"

Detective Hansen then asked if I could meet with him at the station at seven tomorrow morning. I agreed then hung up the phone. The kitchen clock showed that it was twenty minutes past eight. It was not too late. Out the door, across the street, and in front of Old Hank's door. No one answered. Walking around the house, I didn't see anything suspicious. I didn't know what was going on there, but I'd deal with that later. Right now, I have a lot of work to do. It was now two o'clock in the morning. My plans and timelines were final, the designs were drawn. Just a couple of hours of sleep then I needed to get to work.

Early in the morning, I had gathered all of the paperwork together and left the house silently. I drove the Chevy truck to the diner across the street from the city police station. I finished my breakfast and paid for my meal right at seven o'clock. I crossed the street and while walking through the parking lot, Detective Hansen pulled his sedan up alongside me.

"Get in."

We sat in silence, until we turned off of the county highway. We had passed the large intersection where Industrial Way started. I quietly released my breath as we drove right through the intersection. So I guess this has nothing to do about the Impound yard or the Provider Wreckers and Outfitters. A couple of miles up the road, we entered the old huge truck parking yard at the abandoned and dilapidated railroad warehouse complex. This was where my sister was found. Two patrol cars sat side by side. I followed the Detective through a huge opening where the roll-up door was missing. Inside the cavernous structure, several police officers worked with long tape measures, lights, and cameras. Chalk outlines and spilled dark fluids were obvious. Detective Hansen and I were standing side by side watching the police work when the Detective said, "Do you know this man?"

"Yes, that is old Hank, my neighbor." I mournfully stated. "The person you called Hank died right there." Pointing at the far wall where the chalk outline around his body was half on the wall and the other half on the floor. "Mr. Stein was here last night. He waited here patiently and covertly like a good soldier. Did you know he was awarded the Silver Star in World War Two?" I did not. The last thing that Old Hank said was that they would pay dearly. Gunnery Sergeant Henry Louis Stein had kept his army-issued Colt .45 caliber semi-automatic pistol after the war. He was probably just looking around and observing any kind of activity. They probably stumbled into each other. The Detective showed me where the drug dealer stood and where Old Hank was standing when the gun battle started. The four dead drug dealers all had one gunshot wound in the center mass or in other words, the chest. Mr. Stein's Colt held nine rounds. Four bullets in the dead drug dealers and an empty gun in Mr. Stein's hand. No errant .45 caliber holes in the far wall from where Mr. Stein was standing but five bullets unaccounted for. He had a spare fully-loaded clip in his pocket. The Detective brought me very close to Old Hank's body. The medical examiner was still counting the bullet holes in Old Hank's body. Cautioning me not to touch anything, the Detective drew my attention to an area where Old Hank wrote something in his blood. It was hard to see. I looked at the Detective and said, "What is it?"

Detective Hansen shook his head. "We're not sure – yet," he emphasized. I suddenly realized that he wrote the letters **C-O-P** with the last letter, maybe an S. Old Hank wrote it upside down so whoever walked up to him would see the word **'Cops.'** The police were looking at the scribbling in the perspective of Old Hank's. They were taking pictures of the illegible handwriting from behind Old Hank's body.

Stepping back, I walked over to the opposite side of the building and looked outside at the railroad yard. Several decades ago, the land was torn up to retrieve the expensive steel rail, making it impossible to drive up here to the warehouse. Hundreds of acres as far as you could see. The land was totally devastated. What I could see was further in the distance, maybe northwest, about two, maybe three miles, hundreds of crane booms, heavy equipment, and thousands of crushed cars stacked on top of each other.

Detective Hansen stood by my side surveying the rough and broken terrain. "We don't come out here at night," the Detective said, while his eyes were scanning the hundreds of acres. "It is pitch black out here, there are no lights burning for miles."

On the way back, Detective Hansen told me that he has investigated several crimes that seem to somehow or in some way involve me. He asked me if I could tell him what's going on. I honestly answered him, "No, I can't tell you what's going on!"

Back in town, I thanked the Detective for all his help. He dropped me off at the library. With all the new construction and renovation of the old downtown section of the city and county's new administration facilities, everything was all located in this area of town. The new Bureau of Automotive Regulations, or BAR, was just up the street. I presented the state worker with the doctor's letter, authorizing my early application for a state driver's license. The law allowed younger drivers to obtain a driver's license if no other family members were able to drive. Of course, I had to pass the test.

Ten minutes later, I had passed the written test with a one hundred percent score. I was told to wait till after lunch and then I could take the driving test. I took a walk to the rear of the city police station.

Sitting at the bus stop, I read my newspaper and watched every car that came out of the gated employees' parking lot. And just as I thought, the desk sergeant, going to lunch, pulled out in an old Ford four door. Left side fender was dented with a lot of paint loss. Very easy to identify. Back at the diner, I was not hungry so I drove to the BAR and I was first in line for the driving test. With my temporary license in hand, I drove to the hardware and feed store and acquired all the articles on my list. Then a stop at the druggist for Mom's medications. The Gomez sisters and Candi were concerned that I had gone out early without telling anyone.

Looking at their troubled and accusing faces, I told them the truth. "Old Hank is dead," I said while lowering my head. The twins both screamed at the same time. I told them almost everything; some things they didn't need to know about. The Gomez sisters sat on the couch and consoled each other. Tears streamed down Candi's cheeks. Candi and Old Hank shared a love of music that was now lost. I went upstairs to my mom's room and we both worked on a scheduled timetable for her medication regimen. Candi came up and said that the Gomez sisters left and she needed to go too. She kissed us both on the forehead and left. After taking her meds, my mom was asleep in minutes. Downstairs, the old house was eerily silent. Just the creaking sound of the old house settling on its foundation, and the tick-tock of the old regulator clock. It was time to get to work.

I unloaded all the hardware out of my truck and dumped it out on the shop's workbench. Using pieces of scrap copper piping, I had designed a tool similar to a retractable Parker ballpoint pen. The two pieces of pipe were of two different diameters. The smaller piece fits inside the other larger piece of copper pipe. The smaller diameter pipe is longer than the larger diameter pipe. After brazing a sixteen-penny nail to the end of the small pipe, I slid the two pieces together. Then, I brazed a washer to the end of the larger piece of pipe so the nail could slide out but stop at the nail's head. I then slid a long carburetor spring down the small pipe into the larger piece of pipe. The spring bottomed out at the washer. I then slid a bigger washer down the small piece of pipe where it stopped at the top of the larger piece of pipe. Brazing the bigger washer onto the larger piece of pipe and trapping the spring inside. Just like a Parker pen, when I pushed down on the smaller diameter piece of pipe, it retracted into the larger diameter pipe compressing the spring with the nail coming out of the end. When I let the small pipe go, the nail sprang back inside the larger piece of pipe. Done!

I had several magnesium wheel rims that had cracks in them and were in my scrap metal pile. Ones broken into three pieces. With one piece, I had cut away several thin pieces and bounded two bundles of them together with ample amounts of wire. I laid out six party balloons on the workbench. Using a funnel, I partially filled the balloons with gasoline, mixed with used motor oil. The diluted gas wouldn't corrode the rubber, then placing them in a small cardboard box, wedged in with crumpled newspaper so they couldn't move around. I placed the box outside the door, next to a ten inch piece of lead pipe. Looking at my organized mess, I selected a fresh pack of Kent cigarettes with several books of matches. After opening the pack, I lit one and coughed uncontrollably. I hate cigarettes, but everyone smokes these days. Taking a book of matches, I pulled back the cardboard cover and inserted the lit cigarette horizontally behind the rows of matches and slowly closed the book. I set it down on the dirt floor and checked my watch. While I was watching the matchbook, I noticed my hand print in the dirt of the shop floor, which reminded me why I was doing this. The matchbook flared up surprisingly, leaving a heavy sulfur smell. Checking my watch, it took three and a half minutes to ignite the matches. I saw this gimmick in an old war movie. Outside, behind the shop I pulled off an old oilcloth tarpaulin that was covering my Dodge Power Wagon – runs perfect. I never did register it into my name. New tires with a deep and open lug tread design. Got a full tank of gas. I had added another set of headlights, bolted to the front frame. Along with a roof-mounted spotlight with interior manual control handle. This truck is boss! Working to organize all of the tools and devices, I packaged them and placed everything carefully in the truck's lock box. With all steps double-checked, I covered the truck knowing that it was ready. One more silent walk through the house and a peek in my mom's room. All was right in my world.

Driving the Chevy truck with a license made me feel grown up, responsible, or more so, accountable. Having sex with Candi was a starting surprise and an emotional elevation for my male ego. Although for Candi it seemed so natural, like an acquired skill. We both appeared to know what we were doing. We definitely had to do that again real soon.

I arrived at the gate of the City Police Station employees' parking lot and found a parking spot that afforded me an excellent vantage point. I also positioned myself whereas going either north or south would be in my advantage. Just after five o'clock, the old four-door with the dented fender pulled out of the gate and traveled north. I was right behind him. Up a few miles and still in town, we turned right into a track of homes. These newer homes were built cheaply and with very little artistry. After another right, the old Ford pulled into a driveway while I continued on without looking behind me. I made a reconnaissance of the neighborhood and observed that there was only one way in and out of the neighborhood. Parking on the main road just where we made the second right turn coming in, I could see the desk sergeant standing by the car in an adamant conversation with a female wearing a robe. His hand and arm gestures suggested an argument. When I saw him get in the car, I acted quickly and drove up one block, parked at the curb with the other parked cars, and lay down on the bench seat. I reached up and adjusted the rearview mirror so I could see behind me as I was laying down. I heard the desk sergeant's car roll by. Slowly, I raised my head and just looked over the dash, I watched him turn right and roar up the county highway. Here we go.

I was following him a couple of cars back and we'd been on the road for about twenty-five minutes. We were now driving out of our county and were in the foothills. At a wide and slow bend in the road, the old Ford pulled into a large gravel parking lot. As I passed by, I got a quick peek of a rustic single-story lodge. After I completed the slow bend in the road, I pulled over onto the shoulder. When the road was clear, I made a U-turn and returned to the gravel parking lot. As I pulled in, I saw the old Ford parked far over to the left side of the gravel lot. A thick tree line defined the parking lot's boundaries, as though attempting to hide the old Ford. I took a parking spot three vehicles over from the sergeant's car. I had heard about this place. All the young boys at school talked about it like it was a myth. This was the infamous Kit Kat Klub. Crudely described as a topless bar, the sign stated that the establishment referred to itself as a gentlemen's social club. A smaller sign by the door illegally stated "Whites Only". This was truly an opportunity for me. I followed the desk sergeant to accumulate information about his habits, residence, and people he associated with. For him to come to a place like this gave me more than enough information about his morals.

It was now dark and I could blend in with my dark clothing. I popped off the lens of the truck's courtesy light and removed the bulb. Now I could open the door without being seen. Walking up to the old Ford, I ducked down behind his car when a vehicle pulled off the road and into the lot. It was hard to see but the vehicle was a van. Loud country music poured out of it. All the lights and noise instantly stopped when the driver shut down the engine. The two occupants exited the vehicle. Both were large men. The van was hard to see, just a silhouette, but the stance of the vehicle was very high and the tires wide and tall. The men had to hop out of the doors because of the height. One of them let out a rebel yell while entering the club. When all was quiet, I returned to my clandestine operation.

The old Ford was unlocked and filthy. To open the door

would turn on the interior lights, so I left the car untouched. The edge of the half circle-shaped parking lot was ringed with this dense foliage. When the club's front doors were open, the music and light spilled out, warning me of someone approaching. I stepped into the shadows of the tree line and disappeared from their view. This had only happened twice in an hour. The third time it was the desk sergeant. Stumbling a little and searching for his keys, he couldn't see me standing at the edge of the trees right in front of his car. I slid the ten-inch lead pipe out of my back pocket. He came around the rear fender of the old Ford still looking for the ignition key. I stepped out of my shadowy concealment and calmly said, "You got to sign this, asshole."

He came to a dead stop, then recognized me and frowned. The sergeant's inebriated state slowed his reflexes. I brought the lead pipe up over my shoulder and swung down at an angle to my left. The pipe contacted him just below the hairline, on the right side of his head. I dropped the pipe and caught the sergeant as he was falling.

Catching him by his armpits, holding him upright and turning slightly toward the left front fender, I let him go. The sergeant hit the fender head first on the right side just below the hairline.

Performing a half gainer, the sergeant landed face up. I kneeled by his side and removed the retracting nail from my back pocket. While I was waiting for the sergeant to return to his car, I sharpened the nail's edge with a small file. Shaping it into a miniature sword. I carefully placed the tool on the inside of the eye just above the tear duct. Using light pressure, I press down on the plunger's end, thrusting the sharpened nail into the sergeant's brain, severing the connecting tissue of the frontal lobe. After a few small rotations of my wrist, I released the pressure on the plunger's end, retracting the nail back into the pipe with a metallic clink. The sergeant shuddered for just a moment then laid quietly, eyes wide opened. I rolled him over, face down, letting the blood from the cut on his head stream down onto his eyes and face. Still crouching, I moved into the tree line and the shadows. The retracting nail and the ten-inch lead pipe were back in my pocket. Slowly standing and listening, all was quiet except for the sergeant's steady breathing.

Back in my truck and waiting a few more minutes, all was normal. Starting my truck, I backed up with my headlights off. Pulling onto the highway, I turned on my headlight and headed home. I didn't want to kill anyone. So I didn't kill the desk sergeant, I just gave him a lobotomy. I read about it in the medical journals at the school library. I did want to defend and protect my family. The pain and suffering that the desk sergeant inflicted upon my mother and the disrespect toward my dead sister, not to mention the theft and destruction of my mom's car, was an insult that had to be avenged. After about ten minutes of driving, I slowed down, rolled down the window, and threw out the two pipes into a deep ravine. The clock on my dashboard showed the time was ten o'clock. I parked my truck in the side yard in front of the shop.

Copied from spiral notebooks

Chapter 14

In the house, I first checked on my mom. Thinking she was asleep, I turned to leave when she called my name. I was instantly by her bedside. She had just woken and heard me coming into the room. She had a pounding migraine headache and wanted to try the new medication. I had arranged all the pill bottles on her bureau, with the doctor's written instructions. I read aloud the instructions to her so she understood what she was taking. In the bathroom, I filled the water pitcher with fresh cool water and gave my mom a full glass to help take the pills. She didn't need to use the bathroom, nor was she hungry. My mom only wanted a kiss from me and the reassurance that I was there for her. A kiss on the forehead and an "I love you" was just enough to relax her into sleep.

Downstairs, all was the same as I had left it. All the preparations were in place. Time was on my side, enabling me a rest period. Sitting on the old couch, head on a pillow and arms across the chest, I closed my eyes.

I could sense the cold steel nail sliding into my brain. My eyes snapped open. The old regulator clock told me it was three o'clock in the morning. Perfect timing. After checking on Mom and grabbing a pound of fresh ground pork and out the kitchen door I went.

In the shop, I changed into my coveralls and work boots. After pulling the tarpaulin off of the Power Wagon, I double-checked all of my gear. Everything went into cardboard boxes and was packed tightly with crumpled-up pages of newspapers. All of these boxes were carefully placed in the truck's lockbox that was bolted to the bed frame. The last thing to do was to unfasten the battery charger and replace the battery cover. It was difficult not to disturb the silent neighborhood this early in the morning. So, I started the engine and let it sit and idle for a few minutes, allowing the low rumble to lull anyone back to sleep.

With the engine warming up, I put the transmission into gear and slowly navigated my way around the shop, passing my Chevy truck on the gravel driveway and onto the street. Slowly shifting gears and picking up speed, I got two blocks up the street and took a left. I didn't want to drive on the county highway. So, there was a gravel maintenance road running alongside the railroad line and could be accessed down a residential street that I was driving on. I got out of the truck and locked the front hubs then negotiated the dirt berm that kept out any ordinary motor vehicles and hit the gravel road in four-wheel drive.

The road was very rough and had some enormous potholes and gullies that slowed me down. Although the extra headlights revealed potential disaster before any catastrophe manifested. Finally, I arrived at the end of the road. A huge railroad trestle bridge, spanning a tributary that flowed into the Red river. No vehicles could drive on the bridge. There was a tract to the east off the gravel road that led uphill to the county highway. I would have to drive up the hill and use the highway for the next five miles. At the top of the hill crest, I emerged onto a wide shoulder of the county highway and came to a stop. I got out of the cab and unlocked the front hubs.

After driving those five miles, I made the left turn at the big intersection onto Industrial Way. I saw no cars on the highway on the way there. So far so good. Down the Industrial Way to Salvage Road. Halfway up Salvage Road, I slammed on the brakes and skidded around on the slick oily road in a half turn. Now, I was looking back at the way I drove in. Shifting into reverse, I backed up all the way to the gate of the Provider Wrecker's yard. Killing the engine, I sat and waited.

The exhaust manifolds ticked loudly as the casted metal cooled and contracted. I saw shadows of movement behind the locked gate. Jumping out of the truck, the dogs began to bark so I ripped open the butcher paper and fed the dogs small pieces of ground pork. They loved it. They whined a bit when I turned to the truck, opened the tailgate and jumped in the back. Opening the lock box, I placed the cardboard boxes on the tailgate. Back on the ground, I removed a leather tool belt from one of the cardboard boxes and buckled it on. Also, I retrieved a pair of bolt cutters and walked back to the gate. After the heavy Yale lock hit the ground, I hung another exact model on the clasp of the gate, but left it unlocked. The dogs jumped up on my legs and waist. With ground pork in hand, I led the dogs to the truck's cab and got them in, closing the door behind them. They turned to look at me curiously through the truck's windows. With my tool belt full and carrying one of the cardboard boxes, I headed into the wrecker's yard.

When I had first walked in here, I had noticed stacks of old gas tanks, piles of leaking fifty-five-gallon drums, and a large above-ground fuel tank. The fuel tank was a round long barrel about eight feet high on an angled iron frame. The thousands of crushed cars stacked on top of each other in long rows formed a Hundred-Canyon-like terrain. As I was hurrying away from the beady-eyed fat man, feigning fear, I noticed the oil-soaked soil and the little stream of waste and pollution running out the gate and headed straight to the Red river. He should have never threatened my family. There was also some sort of connection with the beady-eyed fat man, the drug dealers at the railroad warehouse, and Bad Brad's gang. No one will threaten my family.

I went straight to the above-ground fuel tank. Setting down the cardboard box and taking out the two magnesium bundles, bound together with wire, I twisted the extra wire of the bundles around the front legs of the above ground fuel tank about two feet from the ground. Then I tied a string from the support beam of the above-ground fuel tank. From that string, I tied a balloon full of gasoline and used motor oil about two feet above the ground next to the magnesium bundle. Once I adjusted it a little and got it just right, I mimicked the setup on the other front leg. From the cardboard box, I placed newspaper pages flat on the ground under the balloons. Crumpled-up newspaper pages were placed directly under the balloons. Magnesium is a soft non-ferrous metal. It burns easily and is very hot. When the heat weakened the angle iron legs, the fuel tank would topple over and explode. The train car that the beady-eyed fat man lived in was just around the next canyon of crushed cars. I had watched for him several times. He had not shown himself maybe because he didn't care or maybe that his enormous girth prohibited general movement. More than likely, he was sleeping very soundly and just hadn't woken up. Whatever the premise, he threatened to kill my family and for that I had no problem defending my loved ones with equal force.

The man in the train car was destroying himself with consumption. He lived in a toxic environment and showed little concern for his health. He'd probably die a slow and agonizing death. I had to avenge my family. Still, he had not shown himself. I had to finish this.

The fifty-five-gallon drums were next. Propping up a pallet against the first drums, I hung the balloons and positioned the newspaper. Lastly was the old car fuel tanks. Cars cannot be crushed with the fuel tanks still attached because of the possibility of compression and explosion. So the tanks are pulled out and piled up to let the fuel evaporate then sold for scrap metal. There were thousands of tanks and probably hundreds of gallons of gasoline still in all of these tanks. Hanging two balloons and placing the newspaper took little time.

Now, the hard part. Back at the above-ground fuel tank, I pulled out of my tool belt, three books of matches. Then out of the tool belt the pack of cigarettes, taking three cigarettes out of the pack and throwing the rest on the ground. I put all three cigarettes in my mouth and with a match I carefully lit all three cigarettes at once. Quickly, I took one cigarette and wedged the cigarette in the matchbook, carefully placing it on top of the crumpled newspaper, then walking to the fifty-five-gallon drums and carefully repeating the performance. Finally, the mountain of gas tanks and I was just a few steps from the gate. With the gate closed, I locked the lock. I needed the lock to be found securing the gate.

I was in the truck with the barking dogs flying down Salvage Road. At the intersection of Salvage and Industrial, I turned right, away from the county highway. The fire would no doubt draw a lot of attention and I did not want to have to explain my presence there. Just as I made my turn, I noticed a light in the north sky. I took the truck out of gear and slowly rolled the truck to stop. I was curious.

The soft red glow was reflecting off the clouds. No, not clouds, but smoke. The soft red glow had grown, now the luminous appearance was undulating, dancing from side to side. The light had intensified, rising, falling, and flashing. Light was reflecting back from the smoke and now I could see the black cloud of smoke rushing up into the darkness. Just a hint, a little flicker. Then again, a little flicker like a fiery tongue licking the sky. Slowly the tongues of flames grew, till the horizon was on fire. The foreground was a jagged inkblot, but beyond that was an intense purity of color. These pure chroma defied the reality that was red or orange. Although hues of various levels of intense greens and impossible deep blues were discernible. Then, within seconds, the intensity diminished to a point that I thought the fire was going out. The fire and light decreased and the smoke column disappeared in the diminishing light. When a fire consumes all the available oxygen or when the fuel overwhelms the temperature of the flames, the fire dies down and the temperature drops until the fire extinguishers itself. This was what I feared had happened.

I needed the high temperature of the fire to completely destroy all my efforts to cause it. A shroud of gloom covered me.

Like a dimmer switch, the dying light gradually intensified. The light took on a curvature appearance that rose as it brightened. Appearing as though the sun was rising. Filling the sky. Turning the night into day. The detonation's shockwave rocked the truck. The explosion consumed the light and left a mushroom cloud. I think that the above-ground fuel tank toppled and spilled gas everywhere, a great amount of liquid smothering the flames. The heat vaporized the gasoline and mixed with the hot smoke rising swiftly. The fire rekindled and ignited the volatile suspended gasses mixed with oxygen in the air. A thermo-barometric pressure in the presence of a flammable vaporish cloud with an ignition source. Burning the air. I was mesmerized.

The huge walls of flame were all-consuming. The dogs were frightened, and so was I. Putting the truck in gear, we got the hell out of there.

I followed the paved road till it ran out. A chipped rock and tar road replaced it. A few more miles and we came upon the immense railway yard. The multiple parallel tracks off the mainline were for parked or stored boxcars, flatcars or tanker cars, usually empty. Hundreds of them were coupled together and parked in random areas. A gang of switchmen were dropped off when there was work needed. They only work in daylight for safety reasons. This was where the road ended. The fire was quite visible and still growing. Turning on the extra headlights, I drove on a wheel tract, following it till the road got too rough. Stopping to lock the hubs, when I opened the door, the dogs flew out. They jumped and barked then disappeared in the dark. I tried to call them back but without any ground pork, their interests were elsewhere. I hoped they liked wild rabbits. Their barking was faint and was coming from the direction of the Red river, away from the fire. After locking the hubs, I started my four-wheel drive escape. This is as far as I got in my Chevy truck when, a few weeks ago, I practiced my escape route to the end of Industrial Way. I found the going hard but negotiable.

The dug-up rails had left the ground with deep ruts and steep mounds. Mocking waves on a dirt sea. On top of one particular tall wave, I stopped and turned on my roof spotlight. I fanned the light from side to side and realized that the mounds and ruts ran along one another. If I put my wheels on the side of a mound then put the other wheels just inside the rut, I could slowly drive at an angular position. I also saw the abandoned railroad warehouse in the far distance with the spotlight. I was headed to the far south end of the warehouses for my escape. The fire had increased in strength and had illuminated my view as though it was a warm summer night with a full moon and a clear sky. After about two miles of that, I emerged at the edge of the broken ground where the trees and low shrubbery were evidence of flat ground. My tires sank in the soft soil as I dodged trees and thick brush.

Within minutes, I came across a well-worn wheel tract heading to a hillock in the direction of the county highway. Now on flat ground, I was covering a great deal of distance away from the fire. On top of the hill, I was given a panoramic view of the abandoned railroad warehouse complex, and the fire that was unimaginably colossal. My view continued with a straight line to the county highway. I saw them before I heard the sirens. Like a red and blue snake, the fire engines twisted and turned with the contour of the roadway. Now was my time to make the final escape, but I had to use the highway for the next five miles. The wheel tract worked its way downhill through a dense cover of trees. It seemed to me that whoever used this crude road knew that the wheel tract couldn't be seen from the county highway.

The last twenty feet was in a creek bed then up a bank onto the shoulder of the highway. No one could have accomplished the excursion I had just completed without a four-wheel drive vehicle with high clearance and heavy lug tires. Somebody else was using this tract. Just before I drove up the bank, I heard the sirens. I jumped out of the truck and peeked over the creek bank. Not seeing any lights, I stood. Climbing up the bank and onto the shoulder, still not seeing a thing. Actually, the sound was fading, moving away from me. I stepped onto the road and looked back at the hillock I had just traversed. No sign of the four-wheel drive tract. The horizon was glowing. This was the time to go. The fire department and police were all at the scene of the fire. I needed to get to the wheel tract that led down to the railroad bridge. But first I needed to drive the five miles of highway without being seen. Back at the truck, I unlocked the front hubs, slammed the door of the cab, and pulled up the bank. I stopped and listened. Nothing.

On the road, I rapidly shifted gears, gathering speed to the best of the truck's abilities. I flew past the large intersection where Industrial Way started. I saw no one. The old truck handled like, well, like an old truck. But it hugged the turns and accelerated in the straightaways. I was getting close.

I drove this tract several times for practice. I also had a bike's fender reflector glued on the roadside edge right where I needed to leave the paved roadway and enter the shoulder. At the hill's edge, the natural incline or degree of angle was about 8% grade of the slope. It was similar to driving off a cliff. I slowed down and left the pavement onto the shoulder. Right at that second, I saw the glow of headlights of a car just before it started into the turn. I instantly killed my lights and downshifted into low gear. The vehicle had just started into the turn when I went off the hill's edge. The heavy truck pitched forward as I stood on the brakes. I thought the truck would slide all the way down the hillside, but the weight of the truck and the deep lugged tires dug into the ground until it eventually came to a grinding and dusty halt. The engine died. Applying the emergency brake allowed me to take my foot off the brake pedal thus extinguishing the brake lights. I sat quietly still, waiting for the concerned shouts, the loud calling out of assistance. The flickering of the flashlight beams, blinding me. Absolutely nothing happened. Whoever it was, they didn't see me and my truck go over the edge. I successfully restarted the engine, releasing the parking brake and shifting into low gear. I turned on the lights and let out the clutch, and started my slow crawl to the bottom of the hill, retracing my route back home.

Parking the Power Wagon behind the shop, I covered the truck with the tarpaulin. Stripping out of my work clothes, I silently entered the house. Everything was the same as I had left it. The old regulator clock showed that the time was five fifty-five in the morning. Sun will be coming up soon. I heard the newspaper hit the front steps. The Gomez sisters would be here soon. So, I started a pot of coffee.

Copied from spiral notebooks

Chapter 15

The Gomez sisters were right on time with bags of meat, vegetables, with baking flour and cornmeal. Before anything with breakfast started, the sisters went to help mom. My mom was clutching a photograph of my sister and crying her eyes out. The twin sisters tried to comfort her but, in the end, they joined in with her. After two hours, the ladies put in their appearance and enjoyed the breakfast Candi and I had prepared.

In the paper and on the local news, it was all about an incredible fire at the auto salvage yards. The fire department could not put the fire out but were able to protect and save the city and county institutions in the vicinity of the fire. The fire was still burning and would be allowed to burn itself out. No lives were lost because lodging was prohibited in industrial zones. Candi showed us all her new Texas Instruments pocket data calculator. Her father bought it to help her at school. I pointed out that she can't use it in class She made a pouty face, then smiled. Just two days before school started, I showed everybody my brand-new, temporary driver's license and explained how it came to be. My mom turned white as a ghost when I subtly mentioned the talk I had with the desk sergeant. I settled everyone's nerves by reassuring them that it will never happen again. The Gomez sisters just had their home's heater and hot water systems totally replaced and were paying to have our home's full heating system completely rebuilt. My protest was shot down by my mom's gracious acceptance. The work would start after we started school. Candi was going shopping for school clothes and was looking for bell-bottom pants and puffy sleeved tie-dyed blouses. The ladies started talking about clothes and apparel. I quietly moved to the kitchen with the newspaper. Oh no, the fire had burnt not only the Provider, but all of the auto salvage yards on the east side of Industrial Way.

"I got to go, but I can wake you up tomorrow morning if you want," Candi said in my ear. I turned to her and kissed her passionately, nodding my head yes.

After Candi left, the Gomez sisters announced that my mom was taking a bath then had to take her medication. I took the hint and went to my shop. On the big workbench, I moved some parts and tools over to the side, laid down and fell into a deep sleep.

The flames were all around me. I flailed and thrashed at the fire, beating the flames away from me. Popping my eyes open only to see the bare light bulb hanging from the ceiling, swinging in a wide arch from being struck in my panic. Had I just had a dream? Looking at my watch, I realized I'd been sleeping for six hours. This was the first time I ever recalled having a dream. It seemed so real. I reached up and caught the swaying light socket, it burned my hand. Was I dreaming about my death? Would I dream again? I'd never felt so exhausted. My body was aching. I'd never needed sleep so desperately. If sleep was my criminal conscience, then I was guilty. I entered the house quietly and slid into my bed. A dreamless sleep.

Candi woke me up for the first day as juniors in high school. Since I was a licensed driver now, I drove Candi to school in my Chevy truck. The school district had adopted a new type of study schedule that divided the classes into two categories. On even days, all students would study at elective or required classes for two periods per class. Three classes per day with lunch and op studies. Then on odd days, students would study at the other required courses or elective classes, with lunch and op studies. So, instead of all six one-hour classes a day crammed down our throats, the students had more time to concentrate and work on projects. Candi and I had dissimilar schedules but at least we could start school together. In the auditorium, all the individual counselors had the class schedule for the students they represented. Ms. Hallikamp, as soon as she saw me, came up to me with open arms and hugged me with genuine grief and sorrow. With tears in her eyes, she apologized for not helping my sister enough. The truth was that when my sister was misbehaving, Ms. Hallikamp was the only one to protect and speak favorably for my sister. She was there for my sister every time, until my sister dropped out of high school. Ms. Hallikamp truly cared and I could feel that in her hug. She is a beautiful person.

Ms. Hallikamp assured me that she would do everything to assist me in any way she possibly could. She went further and explained that I had completed the majority of my required course credits needed to graduate. Also, she informed me that Physical Education was converted from a required subject to an elective class. So, she advised me to drop my elective classes and complete the English 4 and Modern History required credits for this year. Next year as a senior, I could complete the History of American Government required credits, take on a school-sponsored part-time employment experience program and graduate early. Ms. Hallikamp stated that she had spoken to my auto shop teacher who told her that I could probably certify as an automotive mechanic today and was the best teacher's aide he ever had. Ms. Hallikamp hugged me again and congratulated me for being the most intelligent student she had ever worked with. That's when I noticed Candi was standing to the side of us with a big smile on her face. She had heard everything. I asked if I had to drop my electives or could I just keep my schedule as is.

Candi walked to Ms. Hallikamp and hugged her as I was asking the question. "Only you would want to come to school when you could get out of it, Miles, of course you can. All your teachers want you here," Ms. Hallikamp commented on what a beautiful couple we made and wished us the best.

This first day was a minimum day, allocated for scheduling classes' dates, time and location, and issue hall lockers. Candi and I said our goodbyes and went to our first period class.

On my way to my first class, a cute little blonde with green eyes bumped into me.

"Hi, Miles." Upon closer view, I noticed that her eyes were a little sunken in and with dark circles under them. Her skin was dry and pale. Dressed in old jeans and a tight blouse.

I smiled at her and said, "You're the cheerleader, right?"

"Yeah," she said uninterestedly. "You will find a key in your P.E. locker, that's for the locker next to yours.

Everything you need for the rest of the year will be in that locker, OK? It's something for you from Brad."

"Sure," I said without any hesitation. And with that, I rudely walked away from her to my class. Here we go again. After visiting all my classes and turning in my punch cards at each class, I went to find Candi. She was staying at her music class and would get a ride home with one of her friends.

Once I got home, the Gomez sisters told me that the police had called this morning and notified my mom that they had released her daughter's body to a funeral home called Underwood Funeral Chapel. The sisters called the mortuary for my mom and arranged all the preparation. I knew where it was. The Underwood Mortuary was located on the Pleasant Hills cemetery grounds. Just outside of the old part of town, the rows of headstones filled the beautiful green rolling hills. Dad's funeral was paid for by the state and he was buried at this cemetery. Mom, Sister, and I were there. My father was buried with full honors. I hadn't been back there since. I felt ashamed. The Gomez sisters told me in their alternating way that Mom didn't want any services. They told me that after the phone call, my mom had to take extra medicine to cope with her anxieties. My mom wanted me to make sure that everything was cared for.

The Gomez sisters handed me a check from their bank. The check was made out to me for three thousand dollars. After my resistance, the Gomez sisters pleaded with me that that was the only way they could calm my mom down. They assured my mom that all will be done for my sister. They begged me to let them help my mom. The sisters were puffy-eyed and mentally exhausted, they truly loved us and needed to help. They hugged me and in their unison, and sobbing voices, confessed that we were their only family who they loved dearly. I broke down and cried with them, vowing to do anything for my family which included them. They thanked me profusely and after blowing noses and wiping their teary eyes, the sisters told me what they had arranged.

After a shower and changing into my suit and tie, I left to carry out my mom's and the Gomez sisters' wishes. The first task to perform was to cash the Gomez sisters' check at their bank.

The Wachovia Saving and Loan was a new building in the newly reconstructed downtown. It was all glass and chrome, looking like huge blocks stacked on top of one another. The bank shared a two-story parking garage with a cornerstone retail department store. Upon entering the main automatic doors, I encountered a water fountain and features of fine art in canvas and sculptures. White marble floors with huge urns harboring exotic palms and ferns. I had to admit that all of the decor was done in good taste. The employees were well-dressed men sitting at expensive desks and very attractive female tellers tending to several customers. In just a few minutes in line, I was escorted to a desk worker and after presenting the check and my temporary license, the young man and a teller casually counted out three thousand dollars, placed it in an envelope, and handed it to me as though they did it every day. After a pitch to open an account at the bank, I thanked them for their help and walked out with a considerable bulge in my inside coat pocket.

From there, I took a short drive to the city police station. As I entered the main lobby, I was welcomed by the incredibly bright smile of the blue-eyed beautiful. Her name was Toni. She was standing and showing an elderly woman a location on a map of the building. With that done, she turned to me and very professionally asked if she could help me. Smiling back, I replied yes, and asked her out to dinner Saturday night. Her professional showmanship crumbled with her excitement in accepting my offer. We set a time and I got her address to pick her up. After that, I asked about the release forms I needed to sign for my mom. The Gomez sisters helped Mom to arrange for me to sign for her on account of her illness. My sister had already been moved to the mortuary, but before they could prepare my sister for burial, the forms must be completed. I took my copies of the release forms and presented them to the mortuary staff for immediate processing. Toni's co-worker had just returned from her break, so Toni escorted me to the second floor.

In the elevator, Toni hugged me and consoled me for the loss of my sister. She smelt of lavender with a faint scent of soap. She held me very close and I kissed her softly. We separated as the elevator doors opened. Toni took me down the corridor to the County Assessor Office. Once in the office, Toni pointed me to a person at a desk and said, "Goodbye, sir."

So, I replied, "Thank you, ma'am."

After signing multiple documents, there was a two-hundred-dollar charge for the ambulance to transport my sister to the County Hospital. Also, in a homicide, the County Coroner's Department needs a second doctor's signature on the death certificate from a physician not affiliated with the chief coroner's office. At the hospital, the doctor examines the patient and either agrees with the chief coroner and signs the death certificate, or disagrees with the coroner and the investigation continues. The hospital bills the County Assessor Office for three hours minimum for doctors' fees and administration costs. That amount was three hundred and forty-eight dollars and thirty-two cents. I pulled out the envelope from my breast pocket and counted out six one-hundred-dollar bills. Out of the corner of my eyes, I saw the cashier discreetly looking at the contents of the envelope. She counted out my change then signed and time stamped the receipt. She then separated the carbon copies and made three piles. The white or top copy was to be filed by the County Assessor Office. The blue copy was for the mortician's accountant, and the bottom pink copy was for my records. She handed me the blue and pink copies then offered her phony condolences and said her apathetic goodbyes. I thanked her and left.

At the main lobby's desk, I didn't see Toni. Her co-worker said that Toni was loading paper in the TTY's and tele-printers. I politely asked if she had two manila envelopes. I thanked her and placed the paperwork in the two envelopes.

It'd been a long time since I'd been on Central Road heading uptown, passing the breathtaking Victorian mansions on both sides of me and slowly moving up in elevation. These homes were built a hundred years ago on higher ground for protection from flooding. This was before the state planned and devised the water management program for the Red river. Further up the road, the land began to undulate and small hills materialized with white-fenced horse ranches delineating property lines. Single-story long houses dominated the hilltops. The road became a winding serpentine course forcing all drivers to hold onto the steering wheel with both hands. In the distance, the cemetery's tombstones dotted on the hills looked like white stitching on green velvet. I passed through the massive iron gates that were embellished with ornate scrollwork spiraling and coiling around spike-tipped bars. The wide tree-lined boulevard led directly to the Underwood Funeral Chapel. The chapel was more like a Roman temple. Resembling the marble neoclassical Greek Parthenon, but with a central colonnade flanked by wings on both sides, all ringed by Corinthian columns. A great flight of broad stairsteps led the visitors to the portico's huge doors.

Immediately upon entering the mausoleum, obviously there was the office door on the right, it said so on the plaque screwed onto the door. Inside the office, just a few feet from the door, was a counter from wall-to-wall right to left. Behind the counter sitting at the only desk was an impossibly thin man. Engrossed in his work on the typewriter, he held up one hand, index finger pointing straight up while still typing. With a flourish of sweeping gestures, he stood up, pulled the paper out of the typewriter, signed it then put it on a large pile of other papers. I had placed the blue carbon copies from the Assessor's Office on the counter along with the large paper bag the Gomez sisters gave me before I left. He stepped up to the counter and picked up the blue paper file. He took a one-second-glance at the top page, then looked up at me and in real genuine sympathy said, "I am truly sorry for your loss, sir." His voice was serene and passive, like reading a bedtime story to a small child. The nametag on his suit coat pocket read Ken Barlow. His thin neck was dwarfed by the shirt collar and tie. It gave the appearance of the head and neck of a turtle coming out of its shell. The glasses he wore were so thick that from my perspective, they magnified his eyes by two and as he held the blue file, I could see the bones in his hands. Although I saw all these faults in this person, he was the most honest, warm, and sincere friend throughout this whole sad tragedy. From the wall of filing cabinets, Mr. Barlow removed a file and brought it to me. Mr. Barlow pointed out a huge map behind me of the cemetery grounds that he had drawn himself. It was magnificent.

Plot N-602 was where my father's grave was. The closest available plot to my father's grave was N-688. On behalf of Frederica Gomez, he bought this plot from a customer and sold this customer another plot on discount. My sister would now rest one row up and two plots to the east of her father. Just a few steps away from each other. Mr. Barlow went out of his way to broker the purchase of a gravesite for my sister. Then he informed me that Frederica Gomez had instructed Mr. Barlow to use her coffin to bury my sister. Mr. Barlow described the burial chamber as a structure that would last for over one thousand years. This man had worked there all his life. He lived in one of the homes on a hill I saw driving up there. He and his wife of thirty-four years were part owners of the cemetery; she was an Underwood.

Ezekiel Jacob Underwood and his new wife joined the land grab of 1824 to 1826 in this valley. Everyone staked claims for the fertile soil of the low land. E. J. Underwood realized the fertile soil, like Egypt's Nile Delta, was the product of flooding. He claimed land in the upper hill region. No one wanted this region because of the steep terrain and the far distance to water. E. J. found several springs producing clean purified water in the hill region. He then cut down as many hardwood trees as he could reach and sold the timber to the mill. Some of the upper hillside was too steep to safely harvest any trees, so luckily those trees remained. He temporarily leased his land to the cattle barons for grazing land during cattle drives.

Ezekiel Jacob Underwood had amassed a fortune. In ten years, flooding never seen before wiped out everything built in the valley. Hundreds of people died, thousands of livestock lost. Even the gravel road that transversed the valley which is now Main Street, was washed away. Only the dead remained. It is said that E.J. wept for a month as he and his ranch hands gently and respectfully gathered the muddy and mutilated bodies and brought them to the hills. Some of the survivors joined them and helped clean and dress the resting ones.

With salvage lumber and anything they could reuse, coffins were built and graves dug. In the early 1800s, a compass was a very important tool. E. J. used the compass extensively for travel and was one of the tools for surveying. So, he used the compass and geometry to position linear rows with the angular grade to arrange the placement of the gravesites to put things back in order and shed the chaos. Everyone agreed that this was a pleasant place for the resting ones. And so, when there was a death in the valley, the families would bring their resting loved ones to the pleasant hills and E. J. would build the coffin, dig the grave, and perform a service. E. J. knew that the wooden crosses would one day decay so he sectioned the hill into the four quadrants of the compass and wrote down N for north and 1 for the very center of the quadrant. In that space, he wrote his own name for he wanted to rest with all the others that he knew and loved. His family obeyed his wishes, and so if you stand in the center of the mausoleum, at your feet is a magnificent compass cut from granite and inlaid in brass on the north quadrant is N-1. Here lies E. J. Underwood.

After the history lesson, Mr. Barlow got down to brass tacks. In the paper bag that I brought was my sister's prom dress – she'd wear it forever. The cost of the headstone, twelve hundred dollars. Embalming and body preparations, seven hundred and twenty-five dollars. Transportation from the county hospital, two hundred and fifty dollars. Then five hundred and twenty-five dollars for grave prep. The coffin was already paid for, donated by Fannie. Mr. Barlow typed out the bill, then stamped it paid, then gave me the carbon copy and one dollar and sixty-eight cents change. The grave was prepared this morning and as soon as my sister was dressed and interred in the coffin, the burial could start in about an hour.

I asked if I could attend the burial. Mr. Barlow said, "But of course." So, I walked around the cemetery and ended up at my father's grave.

I quietly talked to my dad for a while, then looked at a large pile of dirt one row up. Inside this extra wide grave was a concrete sarcophagus. Hearing an engine running at high idle attracted my attention. I looked up to see a tractor with a backhoe shovel and a flatbed truck carrying a coffin. Mr. Barlow slowly followed the flatbed truck, Bible in hand. The slow funeral march proceeded up the hill to the row where I was standing. Mr. Barlow nodded his head in my direction which I returned and moved to stand by my father's grave. The backhoe lifted the coffin from the truck with straps and moved to the grave. Mr. Barlow joined me, mumbling with his eyes closed, finishing with "amen". As the talented backhoe operator guided the coffin expertly over the sarcophagus, the sunlight brightly reflected off the metallic coffin.

Curiously, I asked Mr. Barlow about the construction of the coffin. "Bronze," Mr. Barlow said in a somber voice.

A bronze coffin encased in a concrete sarcophagus and painted with tar, would preserve my sister's body for one thousand years. This type of burial accommodation was extremely expensive and what Frederica Gomez had arranged for herself, but gave to my sister. Unbelievable, and Mr. Barlow did not comment about the relative expense for these items and service. Unbelievable. In half an hour, the workmen tamped the soil and covered it with sod grass. The headstone's base descended at least two feet into the soil's depth as the backhoe lowered it, while the workmen tamped the soil around it till it was ridged. With the work done, the workmen collected their tools then stood at the grave, removed their varied assortments of hats, and with bowed heads said a silent prayer. On the tombstone was my sister's full name, date of birth and death, and scribed in the polished granite face was written "Forever resting." With tears streaming down his cheeks, Mr. Barlow hugged me with surprising strength and then walked away, handkerchief in hand.

One by one, the workmen, with their hats in hand, shook my hand and expressed their true condolences in Spanish and English. As they descended down the cemetery road, with cloudy eyes, I gazed at my sister's newly-covered grave.

Next to me, my father lay at my feet. Old Hank's bullet-ridden body in front of me. My mom's look of horror when deliberately harassed by the desk sergeant. Bad Brad's threat of harming Candi. All of this fell upon me with the weight of all the world's agony. My resilience snapped, splintered and burst into pieces. Falling. My face in the grass. Pain in my knees. Begging for my dad to help me. Trying to stand. Struggling to breathe. Not wanting to live. Damning all that lives. Remembering the way my sister laughed. Loving my mom and the Gomez sisters. Gulping air, spitting out slobber, and wiping my nose with the coat sleeve. I got mad. I was the one trying to be strong for my family. I needed to be there and stop this madness. I was standing now. Swaying. I said goodbye to my sister and my dad. One last look and a promise to return. Like an old drunk, I staggered down the cemetery road toward my truck, grass stains on the knees of my slacks. Mud on my coat and snot and blood on the sleeve. Don't remember how I got a bloody nose.

Pulling into my driveway, I left my sport coat in the truck and removed my tie. Cleaned my face by using the garden hose. I checked out my impromptu grooming in the side mirror of the Chevy. Padded my face dry with my tie. I didn't like that tie anyway.

Coming though the kitchen door, the two sisters sat at the kitchen table. Looking up at me with their red puffy eyes, they told me all I needed to know. I hugged them both. I told them all was taken care of and humbly thanked them, then placed the carbon copy receipts and a dollar sixty-eight on the table. Upstairs, kneeling at the side of my mom's bed, I whispered into her unconscious ear of the day's events. In my bedroom, I stripped off my clothes and lay on my bed. My world felt weak and weary. My first day as a junior in high school was a day I will never forget.

In the early morning sunrise, with Candi's exhausted naked body on top of mine, I was now fully awake and catching my breath. This sure was a lot better way to wake up than my flip alarm clock. After cleaning up and dressing for school, I was holding my mom's hand and wiping away her tears. Annie quietly entered the bedroom to help my mom into the bathroom and start her day.

Downstairs, Candi and Fannie were talking and giggling while finishing up preparation of a tremendous breakfast.

My concern about my mom's need to get out of bed and be more active was met with an excuse that she had just buried her daughter and was following the doctor's orders. The medication, rest, and relaxation would help her to accept reality and better her health. She just needed love, understanding, and time.

"And we have lots of that," said Annie, as she walked in the kitchen, arms loaded with sheets, blankets, and bed clothes, and headed straight to the washing machine.

Candi persuaded me to drop it and give it time. Of course, she was right, and I conceded. After the delicious breakfast, Candi and I headed to school and got there early. Since Candi was not challenged, she was formally observed as class president in the teacher's lounge early that morning.

With a piano at home, Candi had mastered that instrument phenomenally. In the memory of Old Hank, Candi was working with the small jazz band and playing piano and acoustic guitar. She was editor of the school paper and had had a few articles printed in the country paper.

She also tutored underclassmen in music class and in political science. But probably the most important subject that Candi truly focused on was the Women's Liberation Movement. Like Gloria Steinem, Candi spoke at rallies, city council meetings, and the P.T.A. She would express the need for women's right to birth control and the right to choose the condition of their womb. It was the woman's body, not the politician's. The male chauvinist world must stand aside and grasp the understanding that we are all human beings with the same rights and liberties. Candi accumulated a huge following of young and old human beings. Women and men who agreed by a common consent. She was sought after for speaking engagements and musical performances all over the county. I was not able to attend all of her "gigs" because of my mother's health and my work. Usually, she was gone for the weekend and sometimes longer. There were many occasions when we had no time for each other, but when we were alone together, it seemed as though time vanished. Candi had everything she needed or wanted, but it was never enough, it was never finished, never completed to her utmost degree. Candi had once told me that in her music she wanted to reach immaculate perfection. I then realized she wanted that in everything.

After the end of the simple ceremony in the teachers' lounge, Candi and I went our separate ways to our different interests. It was the fourteenth, so it was an even day and my first period was P.E. On the track while I was qualifying for the Presidential Physical Fitness Award, the higher elevation gave me a full view of the student parking lot. Usually it was not a very interesting sight, but something caught my eye. I slowed down and when it came into full view, I came to a complete stop. What stopped me in my tracks was a van in the parking lot. The body was higher than any other vehicle. With tall and wide tires and front hub locks quantified the vehicle as four-wheel drive. This was the vehicle I saw pull into the Kit Kat Klub the night I gave the desk sergeant a lobotomy. I had to see who was driving this van without them seeing me.

Back at my newly-issued P.E. locker, I found a key hanging on the coat hook. Nonchalantly, I glanced at the lockers next to mine. The locker to the right of me had a lock on it, the one to the left did not. I palmed the key and closed my locker. After a run through the shower, I returned to my locker. I sat the key I found in my locker on the floor. After I had gotten dressed, I closed my locker and sat my briefcase on the bench and dropped my keys on top of the other key I set on the ground. Picking up all of the keys, I open the locker to the right of me. Inside was an envelope and paperwork in the magnetic hidden shelf. All of which I put in my briefcase. With the great number of lockers in the row, no one could possibly realize I had opened two different lockers. My auto shop class and art class were on the opposite end of the student parking lot, so I had no chance to see the van. By the end of the day, the van was gone. Candi was meeting with her cabinet after school so I drove home alone.

Copied from spiral notebooks

Chapter 16

The Volkswagen Bug was parked in the driveway. Pearl and Ronny were in the living room with the Gomez sisters and my mom. My mom looked great, sitting in the big armchair with a silk house coat and silver slippers. Her hair was curled and meticulously pulled into a bun. She was smiling and conversing with everyone in the room. After I hugged and kissed everyone in the room, I settled down on the floor next to Mom, holding her hand. I called Candi, but she wasn't home. Pearl started from the beginning for my benefit.

Pearl's husband's family had lived in Baton Rouge, Louisiana for generations. The family had been restaurateurs since the end of the Civil War. On August 5, 1862, Baton Rouge was liberated and the slaves were declared free citizens. Pearl's husband's great grandmother was officially granted a deed to the property she was living on. She lived right on the river in a small cabin and worked a cooking shed. She had cooked for her master's work crews of over one hundred men. The cooking shed was huge with two twenty-gallon boiling pots, a huge stove, and a meat-smoking pit. The land was right on the banks of the mighty Mississippi River just south of the old State Capitol and the main river docks. Once freed, she cooked for the Union's soldiers and sailors. She treated these young white men like they were her sons. They all loved her. The federal government paid her handsomely. By the end of the war, she had torn down the cabin and built a beautiful home and restaurant on the river front property. For generations, the small family developed and expanded the restaurant to what it was today. Just walking distance from the old and new state capital and several state administrations. The restaurant, called the Cooking Pot, fed hundreds of state workers and dignitaries alike. Pearl's husband was an only child and hated cooking, but loved working with metal. After becoming a certified welder and marrying Pearl, his mother disowned him. Then he got drafted into the Army's Corps of Engineers and was killed in a mortar attack.

So, Pearl finished her long story. Her mother-in-law had recently died from a heart attack. Her will and testimony left everything to her only child. Since Ronny was the only living blood relative, Ronny now owned one of the biggest restaurants, fish market and paddle wheeled hotel and casino in old town Baton Rouge. Pearl told us that the lawyers had been looking for Pearl for over a month and found her at the store two days ago. They gave away everything they owned to their neighbors and were leaving tomorrow morning. Ronny wouldn't give away any of the books, dinosaur drawings, or dioramas. Pearl and Ronny were so sad and so sorry about my sister. We had a going-away party with plenty of food and drink. I walked into the kitchen with a load of dirty dishes in each hand. The sisters were washing dishes and had their backs to us. Pearl asked if I could check the Bug's engine for her, as she gestured a fist with the thumb sticking out and stabbing towards the kitchen rear door. I recognized the seriousness of her look.

"Sure," I calmly said while setting down the dishes and seeing Ronny talking adamantly to my mom in the living room. Just as I got the deck lid opened on the Bug, Pearl touched my shoulder and gently pulled me in the dark shadows of the house. She put her arms around my waist and pulled me in very closely. Her body heat was extremely intense. Our faces were so close, her teeth flashed white in the darkness. Pearl's voice was whispered and husky, she said, "No one knows I took you to the city impound that afternoon, as long as you didn't tell anyone, did you?"

Her eyes got a little wider and teeth flashed. I slowly shook my head no. Leaning forward, I kissed her softly and she kissed me back harder. She reached forward to my crotch, fondling my erection. "If I could fuck you right here, I would, but we can't. You're going to come and visit us real soon. I'll make all the arrangements." With that, she let me go and we stepped back into the light.

"If you torched those scrapyards, I know you would've done it for a very good reason. You come and see me real soon, Miles, OK?"

With that, she kissed me on the cheek and took my hand leading me back into the house.

With a teary goodbye to all, Pearl gave my mom the phone number of the hotel where they'd be staying. Pearl looked right at me when she handed Mom the number and address. I shook Ronny's hand and told him to study hard and go to a college of his choice to learn something he truly loves. As the Volkswagen Beetle disappeared up the streets, we all let out a sigh from our weariness and gave in to slumber.

We're at the school parking lot in the early morning because Candi had a student-teachers' meeting. I told her about Pearl's and Ronny's windfall. She was so excited for them, and stated that they were now millionaires. I dropped her off at the main office entrance and parked my truck in a position where I could see the area where the four-wheel drive van was parked yesterday. I laid down on the truck's bench seats and used an old cracked rear view mirror that I took off my scrap pile to watch the parking lot behind me. The van was dark gray, and looked like it was painted with spray can paint. Dodge had built these new Ram vans, big engine, strong frame, and this one had a raised suspension like my Power Wagon, which is the type of vehicle that can negotiate the off-road trail coming out of the old abandoned railroad warehouse. I could only see the right side of the van, but big Bad Brad stepped around the van with a huge canvas bag slung over his shoulder. The double side doors popped open and three girls and two guys hopped out. One of the girls was the cheerleader I talked to yesterday; I didn't recognize anyone else because of the distance and their movements. In seconds, they turned their backs to me, walking toward the school.

I was not surprised, I thought I recognized his dark silhouette at that strip club. Since the coast was clear, I sat up and sorted out the paperwork I retrieved from my gym locker. Lots of reports, exercises, and several tests all for the first period of fall semester. This was a great deal of effort for me to do all of my schoolwork but Brad's as well, and continue to rebuild engines too. I couldn't help thinking about Pearl's body pressed up hard against mine, her body temperature so hot. I was going to be late for class!

When I pulled up to my gravel driveway, I was blocked by two service trucks, advertising home heating and cooling. The Gomez sisters paid for a new furnace, ductwork, and hot water heater. The workmen had cleared out the basement and piled boxes, bags, and an old trunk in the backyard. I brought all the old storage into the shop, and just out of curiosity, I opened the old trunk. A disintegrating wedding dress and a tuxedo were the first to come out. Dusty bed sheets and several blankets full of holes were at the bottom and hiding a wooden box. In the box was a Smith & Wesson Model 36 .38 special – "Chief's Special" – with a four-inch barrel. The box was felt-lined with cleaning brushes, gun oil, and extra ammo. The gun was clean, oiled, and loaded. This was probably my dad's service revolver. Mom put it in here after he died. Dad would have never put the gun away loaded. I rendered the gun safe. The trunk was literally falling apart, so I dragged it to the scrap pile and stashed the gun in its box behind a toolbox. In a box of old shoes, what I thought was a belt, turned out to be the shoulder holster for the pistol. Trying on the holster, I had to adjust the chest strap but it fit quite well. With the gun in the holster, it felt comfortable; the gun was just below the armpit and easy to reach. With my work coat on, you couldn't see the bulge. Swiftly, I reached in my coat, grabbed the grip, and pulled the gun out to a straight-arm position. Legs apart, knees slightly bent, weight forward on the toes. Thumbing the hammer back. Lining up the forward and rear sights, slowly adding pressure to the trigger – click! This was the gun range training my dad showed me when I was playing with my toy guns many years ago. I needed to go to a secluded place and practice my shooting skills.

There were thirty-two bullets in the wooden box, but I didn't want to be seen buying any more. I'd just have to do the best with what I got. I hid all that I had found and went into the basement to ask stupid questions and get in the worker's way.

Candi had become a well-known person around school and social circles in town, but big bad Brad had become the varsity first-string quarterback even though he was a junior. He had adopted Jimmy Dean's song Big Bad John, changing it to Big Bad Brad. They had edited the song and played it at the games and pep rallies. Posters showed him throwing the football and a schedule of all the upcoming games for the year. I don't follow sports on TV and certainly not high school football. Surprising, I was told that we won the state championship last year. It seemed that the varsity quarterback somehow broke his leg halfway through the season and big bad Brad, second-string quarterback, took the team to the championship game and won.

Candi was scheduled to speak at several of these engagements or maybe I should say games. At our first pep rally, Candi was handed a script to read to the audience from the podium. At the mic, she struggled with the flaky and ridiculous puns to announce the members of the varsity football team starting with Big Bad Brad. After the introduced football team was standing behind Candi, she announced the continuation of the anonymous notes of drug issues to be left in the library. She spoke of women's rights and equality for all, while the jocks behind her made immature sexual gestures, causing the crowd to roar with laughter. Like a pro, Candi finished her short speech early and surrendered the podium to the jocks.

As we left the auditorium, the football jocks were leaning against the auditorium wall. Candi, her friends, and myself walked right by them, heading toward the student parking lot.

"I sure would like a piece of candy!" Big Bad Brad shouted out loud with a smirk on his face and his thumbs hooked in his pockets. He was pumping his hips like Elvis.

At the speed of light, Candi turned on her heels and yelled, "Well, then you'll have to find your dick!"

All the other guys busted out in laughter, but Big Bad Brad turned and punched the closest laughing jock in the chest while hollering, "Shut up!"

I got Candi turned around and heard Big Bad Brad screaming behind me. "That's on you. Whitey, your ass is grass!"

By the time I got Candi home, she had apologized to me for reacting to Big Bad Brad's insulting and childish behavior. I had to ask her why she said "find" his dick. She smiled and told me that the football players were taking an anabolic steroid called Dianabol. These pills were called Dbol and Deca, and were used for increasing muscle mass rapidly. It also shrinks testicles, decreases sperm count, and causes impotency. Some of her friends said that they heard that Big Bad Brad couldn't get it up. It's called a "Deca dick." Candi had humiliated Big Bad Brad in the worst possible way. And in public. We laughed for ten minutes. We kissed each other goodbye. Candi told me her schedule for the weekend and would see me on Monday morning.

At home, everything was chaotic. The workers had replaced all the ducts and made a mess in the house. The Gomez sisters shooed the workers out of the house and were frantically cleaning and dusting the house. Upstairs, Mom was medically fast asleep. I helped the sisters in their cleaning mania and took the non-functioning hoover to my shop. I took the dust bag out that was crammed full. The hose was clogged to the beater bar. No wonder it wasn't working, the suction was lost because no air could circulate. After a good cleaning, I put it back together and brought it back to the house. As I entered through the kitchen door carrying the vacuum cleaner, the Gomez sisters were unboxing a brand-new Kirby Classic vacuum cleaner with all the attachments. The Gomez sisters thought that since they had bought two vacuums last week, and my mom's was broken, that they would give my mom one of theirs. I realized that I had to accept their logic so I took over the assembled one and utilized our new vacuum cleaner.

Saturday afternoon, I called Toni to talk about our date. She was so excited and told me just to come over now. Toni lived in a small cottage behind one of the beautiful Victorian mansions. Just a couple blocks off of Central Road, the mansion sat on a huge lot. The driveway ran along the west side, past the main structure and into the back lot, where the carriage house showed itself off. Lovingly restored with all the elaborate molding and heavy carved ornamental woodwork. The huge carriage doors took up the whole lower floor. Above were leaded glass windows in a diamond pattern. Storm shutters framed the windows on both sides. Toni stood at the far east side of the cottage, behind her a staircase leading to the second floor. The apartment was spectacular. Big living room with fireplace, modern kitchen, and in the bedroom a huge king size brass canopy bed. The bed frame was already there so Toni splurged and bought a box spring and mattress to fit the frame.

Toni had a picnic lunch all prepared with everything, including a wicker basket. We drove up Central Road and turned on a side road that took us to a hilltop. The air smelt of sweet grass and tree leaves. The view was absolutely breathtaking. A short walk took us to a majestic willow tree. Under the wispy and drooping limbs, we sat on a large blanket and ate chicken salad sandwiches, Granny Goose potato chips, and drank root beer. We talked about our first meeting, she loved my clumsiness, and I loved her light-blue eyes.

As I laid back on the blanket, I looked up through the willow's branches and saw several small black birds hopping back and forth, chirping. They were watching us with their small yellow eyes, probably waiting for some crumbs of bread. Is this what we are? Small creatures moving through life, hopping back and forth, waiting for nourishment to fuel our minds and bodies. Could life be as rudimentary, just a simple existence? We made love on the big blanket. The black birds watch us. Then we made love in the big canopy bed, the black birds couldn't see us in here. I got home around four in the morning. As I lay in my bed, I couldn't help feeling that with Candi, sex was a mechanical performance or an automatic function. Her sexual acts seemed well-practiced and skillful. She could apply a condom on me in seconds with one hand. And she was in control of the act completely. When I lost my virginity, I commented about that fact. She did not.

Monday morning, I was up early. I had a pot of coffee going and a cast iron skillet of cottage fries sizzling. Candi quietly entered from the kitchen door. I made scrambled eggs with leftover roast beef, cottage fries, and toasted homemade bread. Freshly squeezed orange juice from the Gomez sisters' tree, and coffee. Candi was ecstatic about her performance in the jazz band. She had excelled with her acquisition of the piano and had developed a style of standing before the piano and dancing while hammering the keys. Her vocals could range from harsh like Janis Joplins, to as angelic as Diana Ross. Candi put on quite a show. I think life is a show to her.

The Gomez sisters made their presence known by bursting through the kitchen door with multiple bags of groceries in their arms. After assisting the sisters with about a ton of food, Candi and I left for school.

First period was P.E., so I was at my locker getting ready when a shadow fell upon me. I turned to look and saw Big Bad Brad standing behind. His left brow was split open and actively bleeding. The left cheek was deeply bruised with visible skin abrasion.

"I got you now, Whitey," Big Bad Brad said just before he hit me in the chest knocking me back into the locker and denting the door. I instinctively brought my arms up to protect my face. The blows rained in on my arms and the side of my head. One especially forceful punch caught me on the side of my jaw, knocking me to the floor between the bench and the base of the lockers. Yelling and shouting from an authoritative voice stopped the assault. I was helped up by coach Vargas, who then sat me down in his office. I spat out the blood in my mouth onto a paper towel. There was a cut inside my mouth from the last punch. I probed it with my tongue – it was not that bad. The Varsity coach and

Mr. Goff walked in and asked about my injuries. I sloughed off their concerns with a wave of my hand. So they started the interrogation by asking for an explanation. I told them exactly what happened. They told me that Big Bad Brad stated that I cold-cocked him from behind and kicked him in the head. Big Bad Brad's statements were corroborated by several witnesses, even though they were all jocks or stoners, loyal and paid-off. I shrugged my shoulders and asked to see my counselor.

Ms. Hallikamp stormed into the nurse's station, red-faced, and pissed off. She had just left a meeting with Principal Gerber and the School District's Superintendent. She had argued in my defense that there were no injuries on my hands, fingers, and knuckles. The bruising on my arms were defensive wounds. That all the witnesses were associates of Big Bad Brad's. And Big Bad Brad was almost twice the size of Miles. Ms. Hallikamp insisted that this was an elaborate hoax and a criminal act. Principal Gerber quoting some witnesses had said that Miles had used a foreign object in the assault, although none was found. The School District's Superintendent read a report to Counselor Hallikamp over the new speaker telephone equipment. The report was about Miles when he was in elementary school. It appeared that Miles had attacked Brad from behind and hit him in the head. This assault was witnessed by two teachers and the vice principal. Miles was formally reprimanded in writing by this very file and suspended for a week. Lenience was given because Miles' father was murdered a year before this incident. Miles was a straight-A student but had no friends and preferred to isolate himself from others. The authorities at that time suggested attentive observation for recurring behavior. The speakerphone picked up the sound of the file closing, indicating that that was that! In defense of Miles, Principal Gerber stated that witnesses claimed that recently Big Bad Brad had insulted the junior class president in public in the most contemptuous way, with Miles in attendance. And for that, Big Bad Bradwill also be reprimanded. Two-week suspension and a written reprimand for both parties in violation of hostile and antagonistic actions on school grounds. And that was final.

I was told that Big Bad Brad trained with the football team during after school hours those weeks. The scandalous gossip went through the school like wildfire. As soon as I walked out of the nurse's station, Candi was waiting. She asked so many questions so quickly that I had to hold my hands up. The nurse had swabbed my mouth with Novocain and packed my mouth with gauze. When I tried to talk, it sounded like I had a mouth full of marbles.

Ms. Hallikamp explained everything to Candi. Candi looked at me in shock. "I did this to you?" Tears sprang from her eyes and she started to cry hysterically. I hugged her as Ms. Hallikamp took us back into the nurse's station and the nurse gave Candi two pills. They looked like some of Mom's pills. I wrote on the small chalkboard in the nurse's office that it wasn't Candi's fault. Big Bad Brad would hit me for any reason at all. His gang routinely punched, hit, slapped, kicked or group-tackled me every week for no reason at all. Ms. Hallikamp was horrified and pissed off all over again. She vowed to put a stop to that immediately, but I warned her that she'd probably make it worse. Ms. Hallikamp told me to go home and she'd write out an excuse slip for me today. My suspension started tomorrow, but if I needed anything, I was to call her anytime. Ms. Hallikamp wrote down her home phone number on the nurse's note paper and handed it to me. Candi would bring me my books and paperwork for the next two weeks. Candi knew I couldn't kiss her with my sore jaw so she kissed me on my forehead and laughed when I made a goofy face.

Copied from spiral notebooks

Chapter 17

As I headed back into town, I spit out the gauze and pulled into the Feed & Seed Emporium. They've got everything, from birdseed to tractors. I bought a one-pound bag of birdseed and drove back to that old and majestic willow tree on top of the hill. I laid down with my light coat rolled up like a pillow and dumped the bag of birdseed all around me. Laying on the soft green grass with a pillow under my head was a comfort I had never felt. The sunlight warming my body with just a gentle breeze kept it cool. As I settled my mind and released the mental and physical pains, I commenced to dwell upon my past and then realized that I was glimpsing into my future. A low darkness slowly surrounded me with a bright light above. Below me, like a mist of dark clouds rolling in, obscuring a beautiful view, and above me the light so bright, one would shield their eyes with their hands. But the contrast was a fulcrum and the slightly teetering balance was a pleasing composition. Floating.

A ticking sound like a clock, called to my attention as though time was here with me. The dark cloud rose and bright light receded to throw off my equilibrium. The light was just a small rectangle now and the dark around me was solid pitch black. Like looking up from the grave. The light left me, so that time and I could rest forever.

My body instantly thrusted forward, sitting me up. The black cloud lifted up instantaneously and soared out over the small valley, twisting and turning in unison. The hundreds of black birds had eaten just about all the birdseed, their beaks making a ticking sound. I scared them off when I suddenly woke up. My watch told me I'd been sleeping for over five hours. And I had dreamed again.

Taking a breath was painful. The bruise on my chest was an ugly yellowish brown. My jaw's injury was more inside than out. The bruises on my forearms were not at all painful and would diminish soon. I thought that when Big Bad Brad punched me in the chest, the force was absorbed by my body's backward motion and the collapsing of the locker door. Big Bad Brad was on the opposite side of the bench and there was distance between the bench and the locker. That distance made Brad lean forward and lose a lot of the forward momentum. If we had been toe to toe, Brad would have probably broken my sternum and my jaw.

During my two-week sabbatical, I built a couple of engines, target practice down by the river, and completed all work assignments and test answers for the midterms. I also completed Big Bad Brad's schoolwork and test answers along with a science report describing ballistic trajectory of a projectile in a flight path. Calculating the distance and angle of the inclination relative to the launching force, the angle of degrees and deflection to arrive at a precise point. In other words, throwing a football. I planned to put it in a toilet in the locker room with his name on it. But on the last day of my suspension, Annie yelled at me that I got a phone call.

It was the cheerleader calling from one of the many payphones on campus. She didn't know what she was getting herself into. Ignorant and naive, I kind of felt sorry for her. The cheerleader told me that this was a message from Big Bad Brad. She giggled when she said that she wrote it all down so she wouldn't forget it; at that point she read out loud my full name, address, and telephone number. Then she read out my social security number, driver's license number, license plate number for the pick-up, and my mom's incinerated car. Also, my dad's, mom's, and sister's full names. Then Candi's whole family names, address, telephone number and vehicle's information. Finally, she said that what happened to Eddie the fat man could happen to anyone. The last sentence she said with bewilderment in her voice. With the sweetest sing-song voice, she said, "Meet me in the library tomorrow morning, OK, bye."

I guess that fat guy's name was Eddie. I knew there was a connection with the scrapyard and Big Bad Brad's drug sales. And now I realized that it went a lot deeper. Old Hank wrote COPS on the floor with his own blood. I bet when he shot those drug dealers, there was a cop in there or someone he recognized as a cop. I wonder if any cops called in sick the day Old Hank was killed. I hated to get Toni involved, but she would be able to quietly find out something helpful. I had to find out who these people were. This threat was real and I needed information to use as a weapon and protect my family. So, after I kissed Candi goodbye and we went our own way to class, I circled back around and headed to the library and sought out the green-eyed cheerleader. She was sitting in the back behind the huge second-story staircase.

With piles of books and binders in front of her, she was intensely engrossed in her work. She looked up and smiled, a pencil piercing her hair bun. "Miles, come sit by me." She patted a chair next to her. We started a conversation about the complexity and sheer volume of studies and schoolwork.

Completing school's mandatory courses and classes was just par. To stand out and be noticed by a college meant a lot of extra credit work and talent. The green-eyed cheerleader was stressed out and physically strained at this extraordinary act of achievement. This was the pallor I saw in her face before, not from drug use but from stress. She wanted to be a children's doctor. She was not Big Bad Brad's girlfriend, on the contrary, she had no boyfriend, she had nothing to do with drugs or jocks. She wanted to be a cheerleader all four years for the popularity and recognition. She was doing this messenger thing because she needed the votes to stay a cheerleader. She was being blackmailed just like myself. She wanted anything I had to give to Brad. I pulled out my study files and pieced together all the typed and stamped schoolwork and test answers from different files and compiled them into one envelope. I handed her the file, and she handed me an envelope.

At first, I was reluctant but she pleaded with me to take it. The cheerleader had a class and asked if I would walk her there. We talked as we walked, and she mentioned knowing about my study group and asked if she could join. I had no problems with that and told her the time and place.

From there, I went straight to the front office. I asked to see Ms. Hallikamp. In ten minutes, she had my new class schedule with P.E. dropped as an elective class. No more locker room bullshit. So, on my even days, I didn't need to be at school till nine thirty, but I was going to be at school early anyway and tutor the green-eyed cheerleader in Math.

I had some time before my next class, so I went to my auto shop class and let my shop teacher know about my schedule change. Volunteering myself to help in his shop class in the morning whenever he needed it. My teacher asked if I could start right now, which made me laugh. During a slowdown in class, I opened the envelope the cheerleader gave me and found a xerox of pictures of my truck parked in my driveway. Then a xerox picture of Candi walking into her house. One more xerox was a picture of the green-eyed cheerleader dancing naked with other naked females. These were poor quality black-and-white xerox copies of expensive Polaroid pictures and were proof that I was being watched. Also, this was the real reason why the green-eyed cheerleader was cooperating with big bad Brad's gang. Although I think big bad Brad was just a pawn in this whole operation.

Now I knew to tread lightly and retaliate in the dark or behind their backs. The one person I felt I could trust was Detective Hansen. Whoever was involved in this, had to know that I killed Eddie the fat man and had knowledge of their criminal enterprise. These people had killed before and would kill again. I needed more information before I went to Detective Hansen. And the only way I knew was through Toni. I couldn't tell her everything, just enough to keep her safe. Since there were no Polaroids of Toni, I assumed they didn't know about her.

On the way home from school, I told Candi about dropping P.E. class. She was so happy and relieved. After dropping Candi off, I drove to the hardware store and used their payphone. I called Toni's house, but no one answered. So I called her office phone number for the first time. She picked up and asked me to please hold before I had a chance to say hello. Minutes later, she came on line with her standard professional greeting. I hurriedly asked her out to dinner knowing she was busy. She let out a long breath, signifying a hectic day, and asked if she could cook for me.

When I arrived at her cottage house, the smell of the spaghetti sauce was unbelievable. She also made a balsamic vinaigrette salad. I brought the French bread. The sauce wasn't ready yet so we engaged in a much-needed activity to help us relax. I think I was in love with this woman. After dinner, she put on the album Young Blood, by Jesse Colin Young and we sat on the sofa and talked. Toni knew a lot about my sister, my dad, and my mom. We talked about my sister's murder. Then I showed her the tickets my mom and I received from the desk sergeant. Toni instantly said that the officers were always supposed to print their name, then sign it. She couldn't read the officer's signature. Also, this was written on a parking ticket, not a moving violation form. Both tickets were ripped out of the ticket book, tearing the corner of the ticket where the citation number was. This made it impossible to research the ticket. She said that this was either the worst police work she had ever seen, or intentionally deceptive. I asked her if she knew of any police officers that recently took a leave of absence or left the Department. Her eyebrows went straight up. Three had. One got drunk at a strip club and hit his head getting in his car, another sergeant got the measles from his kids, and an officer had a family emergency and was out of town. None were work-related injuries, so no paperwork was necessary. There was nothing to look up. Toni explained that part of her job was to maintain the telephones, telex, and tele-printers. Everything came through the tele-printer and was chronologically recorded and time-stamped to the tenth of a second.

Toni and two others loaded paper in all the printing machines and pulled the "info" paper every hour. Some info was printed and some was 10-code. All calls, reports, forms, records, and dockets were telexed or tele-printed and filed by timestamp.

"We can see everything, but there's so much 'info' coming in that we could never read it all. We separate it and box it up so that it can be filed. If you have a time and date, I could look it up. But the incomplete and illegible tickets will be a near impossible task."

If I pushed her too hard for information, she'd want to know why. I woke up at four, dressed, and kissed Toni on the forehead.

At home, I showered, put on fresh clothes and made coffee. With eggs over easy, bacon, toast, and a cup of strong coffee all set on a bed table, I served my mom breakfast in bed and I joined her with my own cup of coffee. And I ate a piece of her bacon. She looked strong and rested. Her eyes were clear and her hugs were strong. Maybe the medication was working. The phone rang which made my mom jump. I soothe my mom's nerves while Annie yelled up at me that Candi was on the phone. She was running late and needed me to pick her up. No problem.

At lunch, Candi's jazz band performed an ad-hoc concert in the quad that sounded right on. She had wheeled out the upright piano from the music room to outside on the upper steps of the quad with the drummer, sax, and guitar on the steps below her. The guitarist was a girl in the school's band, and the guy on the sax was in the school's band too and in the marching band. But the drummer, I'd never seen before.

As the school's day ended, Candi told me that she didn't need a ride home. She'd be tutoring some students in the school band then jamming with her jazz band. When I asked about the drummer, she told me that he was not a student, he was a professional musician she met at a concert. He knew a lot of people in the business and was setting up gigs for the band. This guy looked like he was in his mid-twenties, dark curly hair, tall and lanky, and wore all black with a blank look on his face.

By Friday, after school and in the school parking lot, Candi let me know that she'd be on the road all weekend and that she was taking next week off from school. Candi wrote a song called "The Winding Down." Her band had an audition with a small recording label called Curd Record Co. She'd call me and tell me how it went. I was excited and happy for her. I wished her good luck and gave her a big hug. Holding hands and looking into each other's eyes, without speaking, we saw our lives in the future, worlds apart. Candi kissed me on the cheek, turned and ran to a car where the tall, dark-haired drummer sat in the driver's seat.

Candi had changed a great deal since that day on the bus. Now one day she dressed in a peasant dress with her long straight hair piled atop her head, and then the next in hot pants and a tube top with her long straight hair hanging down to her waist. There were times when I could smell the cigarettes and marijuana smoke on her and other times I could see her pinpoint pupils and erratic behavior. Candi could go from music to women's rights then scream about drug abuse, all in one sentence. At her age, Candi had already lived a lifetime. Broken hearts mend but always leave a scar.

Written while in hospital

Chapter 18

It's been a while since I wrote anything down. With all the sedatives administered by the hospital staff, my tormented and weakened body resisted movement as though I were wearing a full suit of armor. My right lung has been removed. The doctors tried to save one of the three lobes, but an infection in the remains of the damaged lung and the possibility of a sepsis blood infection forced their hand to surgically remove the infective tissue. The doctors closed up the right bronchus tube at the trachea, then returned the ribs and chest muscles to their normal place. My chest was surgically sealed, the secrets inside hidden from all.

Your right lung has three lobes, the left has only two. The left side lung is smaller, to make room for your heart. That's why we use our right hand to cover our hearts during the pledge of allegiance. If I were shot on the left side, my heart would have been torn in half, it would have been instant death. Which, I probably would have preferred. In my weakened state, movement is a challenge that must be defeated. I can rest forever later, I have to finish this now.

Copied from spiral notebooks

Chapter 19

My life continued without Candi. I tutored the green-eyed cheerleader on even day mornings at the library. She saw numbers backward – I think it's called dyslexia. She received an A in English and loved to write poetry and read romance novels. So, I used her strong suit and taught her to write the word below the number. To look at math problems not as confusing and jumbled piles of numbers but orderly sentences asking a question. She thought writing two plus two equals four was silly and giggled about it. It was a beautiful thing when she giggled. Her name was Brenda. After a month or so, Brenda's math skills improved exceptionally. I taught her how to break down information and build outlines to help her memorize. We became friends, even if she was the go-between between Big Bad Brad and me.

I rarely saw Candi unless she performed a concert in the quad or briefly in between classes. Although she did see Brenda and me studying in the library several times and having lunch together in the cafeteria. Brenda and I had shared interests and enjoyed friendly banter, so our relationship had escalated into something much more. I'd been giving Brenda a ride home so she didn't have to ride the bus. Her mom worked late and couldn't pick her up. Her father left the family when she was a child. Brenda invited me to her home several times. We sat together and worked on homework and extra credit assignments.

Out of the blue, Brenda asked me why I hadn't made a pass at her. She said that I was smart, handsome and that I looked like a long haired Steve McQueen. She went on and said that all the girls thought I am cute and some have a crush on me. "Do you think I'm cute, Miles?" she asked shyly. I stared into her beautiful green eyes and told her the truth. I hadn't made a pass at her because I trusted and respected her. That in the envelope she handed me months ago contained a photograph of her and others naked – it looked like a locker room. I choked up describing the murder of my sister, my mom's illness, and the insults she endured all of her life. I began to cry when I explained to her about the Gomez sisters who begged me to include them in my family. I started sobbing when I told her about a widow and her son of a dead soldier, who were left destitute and forgotten by our government because she was a black woman. An environment where the woman's body sold like cars and cigarettes but the advertisers' targeted consumer was a male. Where a man having multiple sexual partners was considered "a man of the world," but a woman's integrity would be considered a whore or slut. I saw women as the nurturing goddess, the stronger gender of our species, who would fight to the death to protect the young from being eaten by the male. I confessed that I loved her, and her incredible and true qualities, and I would die to protect her.

Someday, she'd find a worthy man that would love and respect her as a human being for the rest of her life. By then, I was on the floor sobbing uncontrollably. This was the third time that I'd lost control of my emotions and literally fell apart.

Time stopped, consciousness left me. My sensations numb, as a bright light slowly grew around me. Brenda cradled my head in her lap, gently wiping my face with a warm face towel. For some reason, we were on the floor. She was looking down at me with tears in her eyes, and she said, "You are a worthy man, Miles."

At first, I didn't understand what had happened. I tried to apologize and get up but she held me firm. Brenda said that I was speaking about love and compassion, fell to my knees, and then had a seizure. She held me till I had settled down. She got a towel to wipe my face and then I came to my senses. She said her mother was a nurse and could ask her about it if I wanted. I begged for her forgiveness, telling her that my emotions got away from me. Stress and fatigue had ravaged my strength. I needed to get home and get some sleep. She reluctantly let me go, but passionately kissed and hugged me then told me that she loved me.

At school, she held my hand and leaned against me as we walked. So, we became a couple in the simplest way. Still, Big Bad Brad's gang influenced the cheerleaders to vote Brenda out if she didn't pass on the schoolwork to me. And I continued to provide the test answers knowing that big bad Brad's gang were still capable of harming Candi or Brenda. School is ending in a month and I'll have just one more year and then be rid of all of this.

Brenda was curious about what was in the sealed envelopes that she was passing back and forth. To keep her innocent of the facts, I told her the truth. I was helping Big

Bad Brad with his studies. But Big Bad Brad didn't want anyone to know.

I would stay with Toni when I could. But when she would work a double shift, or if my mom was excited or upset, then we couldn't see each other. Toni understood.

Toni had been over for dinner many times. Everyone loved her. Toni was speaking Italian with the Gomez sisters in the kitchen. I didn't know that her dad was full Italian, and the Gomez sisters sternly let me know that they could speak Italian, French, Spanish, and English. It was good to see my mom up and sociable. There were times when Mom stared off into space or slowly started to nod off. Toni understood and wanted to come over and visit with my mom and the sisters soon, and without me around to mess it up.

With school ending soon, we'd all have plenty of time to enrich our relationship. Ms. Hallikamp called me into her office to sign some papers. Ms. Hallikamp was helping me with my scholarship application. She spoke to my mom on the phone and agreed to help. I was bringing the application home so my mom could sign it. Ms. Hallikamp looked tired, and was possibly in pain. I asked if there was anything I could do for her. She stared at me for a long time, like she was trying to make up her mind, and finally said that she wished she had a son just like me. Then told me that she loved and missed my sister and would do anything to assist my family. Ms. Hallikamp wanted me to get the signed college application back to her as soon as possible. She'd take care of everything. She slowly stood and hugged me. She had lost weight and her hugs were weak. I could just barely hear her whimper. Hugging her back, I whispered in her ear that I loved her too, and thanked her for all that she had done for my family. As I walked out her office door, I looked back and saw her beautiful smile and sad watering eyes. I'll never forget Ms. Hallikamp.

The next week, I had asked at the front office if I could speak with Ms. Hallikamp. I was told that she wasn't in so I left my application at the front office.

The last week of school, Brenda opened the passenger side door of my truck, crying. I was driving Brenda home and trying to calm and soothe her at the same time. So it seemed that Brenda's cheerleader fraternal associates thought that I was a nerd and a dork. If I was Brenda's boyfriend in the senior year, then Brenda would be voted out of the cheerleaders' squad. I told her not to worry. We'd never gone steady. We didn't go on any school dates. We were just helping each other with our studies. I said that it wouldn't bother me, just as long as we stayed friends. OK! That made her smile as she wiped her tearing eyes at the same time.

Now, I could focus my attention on Toni, my mom, and my summer jobs. The Gomez sisters had hired a roofing company to replace our roof and install insulation in the attic. These workers removed the old roof on the first day, insulated and laid out the sheeting the second day, tar papered and cedar shingled the whole roof on the third. I tipped the work crew twenty dollars apiece and thanked them for the new insulation and roof on my workshop too. They started at the Gomez sisters' house the next day.

A month into my summer vacation, I was working on a short block in the workshop with the double garage doors wide open. A new Plymouth Fury II pulled in the driveway. Detective Hansen stepped out of the official sedan, placing his hat on his head and walked into the shop. He was wearing a brand-new fedora. He looked around and nodded his head in approval. I placed my tools on the bench and wiped my hands on an old rag. We shook hands, then with a serious face he asked when was the last time I had seen Candi. The question caught me off guard and I took a couple seconds to respond. I thought about it and said probably two months ago at school.

"Why?" Detective Hansen turned his head away from me so I wouldn't see the expression on his face. I urgently implored Detective Hansen to tell me anything he could. He said Candi had been missing for five days. She had missed two important meetings with a music producer. Her agent called us. We talked to the parents and they admitted to not knowing where she was. Detective Hansen said that he believed me. Then asked me if I did see her to ask her to call him and handed me his card. I assured him that I'd help anyway I can. As he drove away, I noticed that his card was embossed in gold lettering and stated that he was now Chief Detective Hansen.

I heard the newspaper thump against the front door early the next morning. With a full cup of coffee, I sat on the brand-new sofa and read the paper. The Gomez sisters bought the sofa, armchairs, Colored TV and lounge chair. My mom got a brand-new bed. On page three was a story of a female body found in the creek by my old junior high school. That's the area where big bad Brad's gang beat me up for the first time. Chief Detective Hansen called me that afternoon and asked me if I could come in and talk to him. The first thing I did was call Toni. She was at work, so I made it short. I would tell her the rest when she got off of work.

A uniformed police officer was waiting for me in the lobby. Toni and I didn't make eye contact. The elevator ride was sterile and silent. The squad room was busy and full of desks with men and women working at them. Telephones, typewriters, and people talking flooded the large space. Interrogation rooms lined one wall, window-framed offices lined the other. Sitting in a chair and talking to an officer was Candi's father. An older man with tousled hair and clothes came out of an office with Chief Detective Hansen behind him. With a hand gesture, the Chief Detective beckoned me into the office. Chief Detective Hansen was all business. He told me that I had the right to not answer his questions, and the right to have my parents in the room while being questioned. I declined my privileges and offered my participation in any way I could. Chief Detective Hansen thanked me, then asked me, for the time being, not to divulge our conversation to anyone. I agreed. After a preliminary dental examination, the body found in the creek was Candi's. She had been raped, beaten, and stabbed in the heart. Wrapped in a weighted-down canvas tarpaulin and thrown in a deep pool of the creek. The bloated body escaped its anchor and floated downstream to shallower water. An elderly man found her when he was fishing for crawdads yesterday evening. He asked if Candi was my girlfriend.

"She was until about six months ago," I stated.

He asked if I have ever had sex with her. I answered yes.

He inquired about other males that were having sex with Candi that I knew about. I explained our break-up and the presence of the lanky dark-haired drummer. The next question floored me. Chief Detective Hansen asked if I fathered a child with Candi. I demanded to know what he's talking about. The Chief Detective reminded me that I had agreed not to repeat our conversation to anyone. I concurred. The medical examiner found evidence in Candi's body of a pregnancy and natural childbirth, maybe two years ago. I assured him that I was not the father. Candi and I started our sexual relationship less than a year ago and always used a prophylactic. The Chief Detective asked if I recognized the man who walked out of the office just before I walked in. No, I had never seen that person before. Out of emotional desperation, the Chief Detective asked if I had any idea who killed Candi.

Big bad Brad had only threatened to harm Candi but not kill her. "No," and that was not a lie.

I had to ask about the tousle-haired man that Chief Detective Hansen had just mentioned and had interviewed before me. Evidently, he was a music teacher in a private school that Candi had attended a year and a half ago. The music teacher had been caught in Candi's bed, naked. With no explanation. He had been fired but no charges were brought against him by Candi's family. Chief Detective Hansen apologized for the confidential questioning. He knew I had nothing to do with this grim act. We were looking right in each other's eyes when he asked me if I had anything to tell him, anything. He was reading me and saw something. I did have something to tell him, something. So, I did.

"Sir, I have a system of studying subjects for school. I have utilized this system in examining the rapid growth of the drug issue in this county. I have compiled facts, information, and personal observation. With this accumulated data, I constructed an outline and a timeline. Once I had all the information in place, there were holes and blank spaces left in my outline. From there I had to investigate the 'who, what, where, and why' to fill in those blanks."

"In my summary, I theorized that some people in positions with law enforcement, U.S. and Mexican government and management within the railroad industry are responsible for this drug epidemic. The type of pharmaceutical drugs available on the black market are not manufactured in the United States. Pharmaceutical drugs like diet pills and steroids are manufactured and legally sold in Mexico, but are regulated in the U.S. and are sold in the growing black market. Illegal drugs like marijuana and cocaine are imported to Mexico from South American countries.

"By law, the railroad industry cannot lock their boxcars. For fire safety reasons, the boxcars have heavy metal seals with serial numbers stamped on them. The boxcars have registration numbers painted on all four sides and top for identification of cargo. A syndication in Mexico is using the railroad industry to transfer illegal drugs into the southern states. It's probably coming out of the railroad hub in Laredo. The parties in Mexico that are responsible for these criminal acts are giving their American counterparts information about the registration numbers of the boxcars that contain contraband. Alcohol and cigarettes are also stolen out of boxcars but before the state's tax stamp has been applied. They probably open other boxcars randomly to deceive their true targets. Certain corrupt managers at the railroad offices schedule the boxcars to be parked in the rail yard at the end of Industrial Road and are broken into at night.

"With specially modified vehicles, they transport the drugs and stolen items to the old abandoned railroad warehouse where they distribute it to buyers. The auto salvage yards would provide a concealed storage site. Large caches of drugs and money could be hidden in scrap cars and transported by flatbed truck anywhere in the state. The fire could have been an accident during their activities, or retaliation. There are probably people in our county police department who know about these illegal activities and are assisting the dealers. The day after Henry Louis Stein was murdered, two police officers called in sick, neither have returned. They were shot by Mr. Stein. They probably didn't die, but couldn't let their wounds be known. Mr. Stein recognized one or both of them and shot them. Before he died, he tried to write COPS, in his own blood.

"I feel that there are some very influential and powerful governing individuals who are dealing with millions of dollars in cash from the drug sales. You can't go to your corner bank and deposit a million dollars in cash. The federal government would want to know where the money came from. Unless illegal cash money was invested in large construction projects and absorbed with legitimate funds. When the drug problem started, downtown began its renovation. In the past three years, several big construction projects have been completed along with many more in various stages of completion. A multitude of businesses, suppliers, and subcontractors, along with some of the largest construction companies in the nation and finally a small army of architects with thousands of blueprints, are making a fortune with these contracts. This is a perfect environment to use dirty drug money and receive clean and legal returns from their investments. The true problem is, this is so involved and political that you cannot do anything about it, sir."

He asked if I could give him my outline. I agreed but warned him to be careful who he showed it to. He thanked me for my help and would meet me for lunch tomorrow where I could give him the outline. He also offered me a job after I graduated.

Coming out of Chief Detective Hansen's office, I saw Candi's dad was standing at a desk. He seemed agitated. He was yelling, "No, I won't," to an officer as he looked up at me.

"You did this," he sneered as he rounded the desk and headed straight for me. "You put all those ideas in her head, you killed her!" he screamed as he grabbed my throat. I grabbed his little finger and bent it back. He whimpered and fell to his knees. He was drunk. I could smell it on him. I let go of his finger.

He screamed hysterically. "You're the one who killed her, you bastard, I'll kill you!" He sniveled on the floor, tears streaming down his face, snot running out his nose.

In an instant it all became clear to me. Candi was gone for over three months in the summer, filling out with a bounce in her step. Staying home to help her mom with her baby brother. And it came right out of my mouth. "That's not Candi's brother, that's her son!" I yelled it in his face. "And you're the father, you son of a bitch, maybe I'm going to kill you!" I screamed with spittle flying out of my mouth. He scurried to his feet and wept as he left in haste.

Absolutely everyone in the office heard the exchange and were stunned and staring at me. Chief Detective Hansen invited me back into his office. I told him of my suspicion about the baby. The Chief Detective was going to order blood tests of the whole family. On my way out, Toni let me know that she was working a double shift tonight and would call me tomorrow.

As I was driving home, a fire truck passed me. When I turned down my street, I could see a smoke column rising up above the trees. Following the smoke, I found myself in front of Candi's home. Candi's dad's Cadillac was a ball of fire sitting in the driveway. The firemen had just hooked up a hose to a convenient hydrant and fought the car fire. The front door was wide open so a uniformed officer and two firemen rushed in. Seconds later, one of the firemen came out with, what I know now, was Candi's baby boy. The baby was crying but didn't seem to be injured. The cop came out and yelled at the other cops and all the firemen to move those people back across the street NOW! One of the new Ford E-Series ambulances came screaming down the road and skidded to a stop in front of the house, giving a wide berth to the burnt-out Cadillac. All of us spectators were on the other side of the street and couldn't see anything. The firemen were satisfied with their work and stowed their gear and left. They made room for another ambulance and two more squad cars.

Ten minutes later, a new Plymouth Fury II pulled up to the curb. Chief Detective Hansen walked quickly up to the house. A uniformed officer was guarding the door, but urgently ushered him in. Ambulance crews and uniformed officers were coming and going for over an hour before I saw Chief Detective Hansen again. I got his attention and he beckoned me over. He sat in the Fury and opened the passenger's door. The car smelled new and had a police radio.

Chief Detective Hansen looking through the windshield at the house said dryly, "He killed his wife and himself, he put the baby in the crib with a bottle. Probably set fire to the car to get our attention and find the baby."

Candi's dad was dead, and I killed him with the truth. Chief Detective Hansen told me that Candi's mom kept a secret journal that told a story of Candi's sexual manipulation of her father, and how she controlled everyone in the house. She would order her father to beat her mother to maintain her power. Candi used sex to get what she wanted in life. Candi's adoption papers were also in the journal. And that probably caused her death. I assured the Chief Detective that I would not tell anyone about our talk. By the time I got home, dinner was ready but I had no appetite. That night in my bed, I thought of Candi, the haunting music of her violin, the fierceness in her women's lib speeches, and the passion in her love-making. I cried like a baby till sleep took me.

In the morning, most of the story was in the newspapers and the TV news. Even the network news carried the story with David Brinkley. Candi's song "The Winding Down" would be recorded on a 45 and a jazz jam with Candi's piano solo on the flip side.

The Gomez sisters and I deliberately kept the sad news from my mom. Toni understood and was helping me through this tragic and shocking affair.

When the sheet fell off my sister's chest, I saw a wide gaping wound in between her breasts. Chief Detective Hansen said Candi was stabbed in the heart. It would take a man with great strength to plunge a knife through bone and flesh then penetrate the tough fibrous muscle of the heart. Even more, a man who cared so little about another's life. A sadistic and mentally deranged person full of hatred and drugs. Candi's dad had none of those things. He loved her and his son. The drummer and the music teacher were weak and cowards. They had no reason to commit such an atrocity. Big bad Brad had a reason. He had brute strength and abandoned insanity. He killed Candi and my sister. I was sure he killed others like Trevor. It was time for him to pay for what he'd done, not just to me, but many others too.

The first day of school as a senior, I headed straight to the front office to talk with Ms. Hallikamp. The office administrator told me that Ms. Hallikamp was not here. Mr. Gerber was filling in for her. I had her phone number, so I called her on the payphone right outside the office. No one answered, it ranged many times. I was told I could go right into his office. Mr. Gerber was cordial but would not talk about Ms. Hallikamp. I told him she was helping me complete my scholarship paperwork. The forms were signed and were in Ms. Hallikamp's hands at the end of school last year. Mr. Gerber genuinely had no idea that Ms. Hallikamp was assisting me. He hadn't seen my application. Mr. Gerber had all of Ms. Hallikamp's files brought to his office. He worked on these files all summer; he'd been through all the files, some twice. I implored him to call her and ask if she recalled what happened to my scholarship application. Mr. Gerber told me that he couldn't do that. I begged him to maybe send her a letter, anything. Looking me in the eye, Mr. Gerber said that he couldn't tell her anything.

"Miles, Ms. Hallikamp passed away two months ago. She had cancer, Miles, maybe you can help me and keep it a secret for now, OK?"

I was devastated. Ms. Hallikamp meant so much to me. She had such a kind heart. I wished she could have been my mom. I felt so sad, like being lost in an unfamiliar crowd. Mr. Gerber gave me the blank forms to fill out and file. That was all he could do.

It was a minimum day so I was issued a locker, then went to each class for fifteen-minute oration and turned in my punch cards. In tribute to Candi, a shrine was built in the quad where she would play her violin. Everyone expressed sorrow and comforted me the best they could. I was out of there by noon. At home, the scholarship application turned out to be harder than I thought. School-issued documents were needed along with teachers and staff's written recommendations. Even then it had to be approved by the principal's signature and confirmed by the School District's Superintendent. On top of all that, time was very limited. But it was not impossible, I would ask my teachers for support. I needed my scholastic history issued by the school's staff. I'd fill out the forms the best I could then have my mom sign it and of course my own signature. I just had to focus on the task at hand and not panic. The next morning, I made an appointment with the front office to acquire my grade history and to talk with Mr. Gerber.

Next, I visited my newly-issued locker to drop off some of my school stuff. Once I got the locker door open, I realized something was wrong. A large paper-filled white binder sat on the locker shelf. Behind me, I heard a familiar voice.

"What do we have here, Miles?" It was Mr. Goff, and he was standing right behind me. Putting his left hand on the inside of the locker door and leaning on it, forcing the door completely open. I backed up away from the locker without speaking. Mr. Goff reached in and pulled out the binder, which was the only item in the locker. With a low-toned whistle, Mr. Goff flipped through the paperwork. "Where did you get all of this, Miles?" I didn't say a word to this asshole, but I did flip him the bird. He angrily snapped the binder closed and grabbed my forearm. I very quickly grabbed his wrist and rotated my forearm back toward him, bending his wrist. Mr. Goff let out a yell, dropped the binder, and grabbed my hand. I bent his wrist further back and down, bringing him to his knees. I leaned in forward, my mouth close to his ear, and said, "Tell Brad that I know." Then I let him go.

Sitting in front of Mr. Gerber's desk, I had to face the music. The binder contained all the first semester tests, examination, and final studies. Also names, addresses, and phone numbers for teachers and staff. And some staff and students' personal files. Among the students' files were Candi's and Big Bad Brad's. Some of the staff's files were Mr. Gerber's and Mr. Goff's. Mr. Gerber was seething, and demanded an answer to explain these outrageous accusations. I calmly stated that my fingerprints were not on the binder and this morning was the first time I had ever opened that locker. Someone else put it in the locker and told Mr. Goff to be there this morning and bust me.

"Who would put the binder in your locker? And why!" Mr. Gerber yelled.

This was a direct question. Mr. Gerber was truly upset. I don't think he was involved in this. I had never lied. And I was not going to start. So, I told Mr. Gerber the truth. Big bad Brad had the binder put in the locker. He had been extorting me to answer all the questions and return the paperwork for three years. There were people in the front office who were passing this paperwork off to his gang. Employees at this school who were helping his gang cheat, like some coaches and Mr. Goff.

Mr. Goff exploded, "Fuck you, punk!" as he leaped out of his chair. Mr. Gerber stopped him coldly and ordered him out of the office. Mr. Gerber silently stared at me for a few seconds, then asked me about the extortion. I told him Big Bad Brad threatened to harm Candi and myself. Now she'd been murdered and I was being accused of cheating on tests.

"I can't just let this go, Miles," he said at the same time his phone buzzed. It was the School District's Superintendent; Mr. Gerber put the call on the speakerphone. The Super had already talked with Mr. Goff. He said that I was expelled from school and that the last college scholarship grant would be awarded to Brad. Mr. Gerber reminded the Super that cheating on a test was a minor offense. I couldn't be expelled for that. The Super argued that I was in the possession of staff personnel records. Mr. Gerber commented that someone from the office gave away that paperwork, and that would start off a big investigation. That wouldn't look good for the Super's public office campaign next year. The two men parried for a few minutes trading off insults and threats till Mr. Gerber hung up on the Super. Mr. Gerber stood up for me, so now I just got a three weeks' suspension. There was nothing to be done about my college grant, the Super had the last word on that. Mr. Gerber reluctantly said that at least I'd get my high school diploma. I thanked him for his help and begged his pardon for all the problems and offenses I had caused.

Mr. Gerber looked at me, his face red, with sweat trickling down his baldpate and pinching the bridge of his nose. He said, "This job's a real bummer, I'm quitting at the end of this year. Just try to stay out of trouble for the rest of the year so both of us can get out of here in one piece, OK?" I agreed and left with my head in my hands.

Working my way through college would take me a decade and cost me tens of thousands of dollars. My chance to win a college grant was lost to a nitwit that I helped to steal it from me. With his athletic abilities and my grade point average, he'd skip right through four years of college football then play pro football and get rich. What had I done? My sister and Candi with a hole in their hearts and six feet in the ground. My struggle and hard work was thrown away like trash. That bastard Big Bad Brad set me up, killed what I loved, and had stolen my life. I needed time to plan a course of action and take back all that was rightfully mine. And then to destroy the one thing that Brad loved, his body. He would never walk or have the use of his arms. With a small hand ax, his spine would be severed. I could hurl him in his van off a cliff on the country road to cover my deception. He would live, but just barely. He would know pain and suffering for a lifetime. And be constantly reminded of his atrocities.

Now, with three weeks off, I could concentrate and work on a new project and start healing my assaulted mind. I'd say nothing to Toni or my mom or the sisters about my suspension. I could intercept the school's letter and sign it myself then return it. I had only two classes a day on the odd/even schedule. So I was home by noon anyway. I was going to take Ms. Hallikamp's advice and take the school's sponsored employment experience program. I'd get a job working as a mechanic for an engine repair shop. Saving money for my financial college future. School in the morning, work from noon till night, and eat and sleep in between.

In the wee hours of the morning, while I was working on my studies, I thought I heard a low mournful groan. The humid air hung still, the sound traveled unhindered. A wail uttered in absolute sorrow and intolerable pain rose to an unbelievably high pitch. I stood and leaned forward on my desk to get a better look up the street. A loud crash followed by a cry in pain. By this time, I had the window wide open. I was lying on the desk with my head out the window. Out of the darkness, a phantom appeared running toward me. Howling like a banshee, the ghost-like figure ran right below me. The gray hair windswept back, the white nightgown flapping and fluttering in the breeze as she went by. It was Annie, and something was not right.

By the time I caught up with her, we were a block and a half down the street. Fighting me all the way till I got her into the house. Thankfully, my mom was already on the phone with the police, so I told her to ask for an ambulance too. By the time the police arrived, Annie was a puddle of tears. She was unable to speak. I directed them to Fannie's and Annie's home next door. I stayed outside as they investigated inside the house. An ambulance pulled up to me asking where they were needed. As I was leading them to Annie, one of the police officers coming out of the sisters' house shouted for help. The medics ran toward the frantic cop and disappeared inside. Something was very wrong yet I knew what it was. I went back into the house to help my mom with Annie. They were crying, their faces buried in each other's shoulders. One of the cops came in to ask Annie some questions. She was inconsolable. I answered the basic ones, then I asked him what was happening. He stated that the lady of the house had died in her sleep. Annie raised her head up and howled insanely. Seeing Annie's face for the first time, the young police officer stumbled backwards, tripping over the end table and falling onto the floor. A look of sheer terror on his face. I forgot to tell him that Annie was the identical twin sister of the deceased. Oops.

The ambulance team attended to Annie and loaded her in the ambulance. My mom stood at the threshold of the front door watching, while clutching the front of her silk house coat. Next door, the police guarded the house awaiting the coroner. I guessed that Fannie died in her sleep and Annie found her. The shock was too much for her to bear. She became confused and deranged, she was running to get help. I believe that Fannie and Annie have been together all of their lives. I mean in close proximity even after their birth. They had never been away from each other, ever. Not until tonight, when Annie went to the hospital and Fannie was going to the morgue.

That morning, I brought my mom breakfast in bed. She was lethargic and exhausted. I got her sitting up and helped her with the two-minute egg. I also made honey buttered toast and a small bowl of wheat hearts. I told her of my plans.

"I'm going to the hospital to see Annie. I'll find out when she will be released and bring her home. Then I will find out when Fannie's body can be moved to the Pleasant Hills Cemetery, where she can rest forever."

My mom said she could not go but she'd be fine by herself. At the hospital, I was directed to the far wing and to inquire at the front desk. I was asked if I was a family member. I spoke truthfully and said, "Yes. I am the sisters' only family." They told me to go to the waiting room and someone would be with me shortly.

After an hour, I asked about Annie again. I was again told to wait. Finally, a very handsomely dressed gray-haired gentleman introduced himself. He was an envoy, part of a diplomatic team from New York. They were here to assist the Spanish government and protect the countesses. The agent wanted to know what kind of relationship I had with the countesses. After I had given him a detailed and extensive family history, the agent showed mercy on me and gave me some real family history.

Luis Gomez-Acebo was Duke of Badajoz and Viscount de la Torre. This was the countesses' grandfather. Their father held the title of Duke before he ran off to America. But in the war, he fought heroically and was awarded the Silver Star with oak leaf cluster for gallantry in action and the saving of many lives. After the war, the Spanish Royal Family invited the Duchess and her daughters back to Spain and to their place of royalty. She declined. When the countesses reached the age of eighteen, they could choose for themselves. And I knew the rest of the story. The family had been receiving their percentage of the royal family's proportion for decades. He then told me that Frederica would be flown to Spain and buried with the royal family. Alejandra was heavily sedated. When she was healthy enough to travel, she'd return to Spain for extensive mental treatment. I asked if I could say goodbye but the agent shook his head and said that I couldn't see her. The Spanish people want their countesses back and will care for them forever.

As I left the hospital, I couldn't help but feel that I had lost so much while the people around me gained something or were being cared for forever. Oh well, I needed to get back home and take care of my mom.

A week and a half into my suspension, and it was like I had accomplished nothing. The next morning, I was mowing the front lawn when the mailman handed me the mail. The sisters and my mom had handled the household financial necessities for years. I stuck the letters in my back pocket. Just as I was sitting down for lunch, I felt the long-forgotten mail in my back pocket crumpling. I fished it out of my pocket and tossed it on the kitchen counter with about a week's worth of other mail. It wasn't until the next day when the mailman dropped off the daily mail in our letterbox that I remembered all the mail on the kitchen counter.

After making dinner, cleaning the kitchen, and drawing a bath for my mom, I sat down with the week old mail. A few advertisements, bills, and coupons. A letter from Wachovia Bank to the Gomez sisters, but with my mom's address on it, fell in my lap. I opened it and stared at the bill. The bank was billing the sisters' account. The sisters' checking and investment account was liquidated, and over ten million dollars was transferred to the Royal Bank of Spain. The transfer went through before the final payment for the house and property taxes were received. A total bill of over twenty thousand dollars was due by the end of the month. The house in question was my mom's.

The next morning, I brought my mom breakfast in bed. We talked as she drank her coffee and ate her one-eyed sandwich. I nonchalantly asked her about the bill. She told me that a year or so ago, the Gomez sisters had bought the house from my mom. The sisters invested my mom's money in their investment account. They then leased the house back to my mom with the invested money. What the Gomez sisters did was to buy my mom's house, invest my mom's money in the sisters' investment account, and use some of it to pay a lease and taxes in my mom's name. In a sense, they were going to give my mom her house back and the investment money. With the new furnace, roof, and paint plus all the furniture, all paid by the sisters so that my mom and the Gomez sisters could live there for the rest of their lives.

I remembered that the sisters had said they would do anything for us. My mom said that my father's pension was a lump-sum payment and that it was all gone. Just the social security payments, which the sisters put in their bank account. Maybe a couple of hundred dollars was all she thought she had in her old bank account. Today was the beginning of the weekend. I'd have to go to the bank on Monday morning at ten o'clock, which was the end of the month.

Monday morning, and after an hour of waiting, the vice president of the bank asked me to follow him. Through the huge wooden double doors, we entered a spacious office with a wall of leather-bound books, tasteful paintings, and bronze statues. The vice president didn't mince his words.

First, he criticized me for opening the letter I brought with me. He then placed a document in front of me. With a very expensive Mont Blanc pen, he pointed at the name on the paper and asked, "Is this your mother's name?"

"Yes, sir," I answered.

"Is this her signature?" He again pointed with the gold pen to the bottom of the lease document.

"Yes, sir." He then asked why my mother wasn't here. After I told him that she was ill, he shook his head with disconcert.

He dryly stated that the Gomez account had made all the payments on this lease. "Since the Gomez account was closed and liquidated, it's evident that no more payments will come from that account. After a financial investigation of your mother's accounts, we feel it's best to foreclose on this lease. We are also seizing all properties of value in your mother's name." He pointed at the lease where the penalties were described. He silently laid in front of me the court order for impoundment of estate, properties, accounts, and vehicles. "You have two days to gather your personal items and vacate the premises." He then gathered all the papers in front of me, placed them in a file folder and handed them to me. "Your copies, sir, good day." If I had my gun on me, I would have shot this bastard between the eyes, but...

Instantly, the huge wooden office doors opened and a tall, barrel-chested and crew-cut man in a suit, held the door open and gestured for me to leave. I suppressed all of my anger and walked out of there with my head held high. I saw on the court order that the two vehicles and my bank account were included in the foreclosure. My mom's name was on the registrations and on my joint bank account. Everything was gone. Although they were going to have a hard time getting my mom's car. I left my truck in the parking garage and walked around downtown. Contemplating my options, I found that I had wandered to the diner across the street from the city police station. I bought a newspaper and a cup of coffee and waited for lunchtime.

Before I left the diner, I called my mom to check on her and told her I would be home soon. Then I crossed the street and took Toni to lunch. I told her about the banking fiasco, but I couldn't blame anyone. The Gomez sisters were trying to help my mom and would have if Fannie hadn't died. I was going to ask Pearl if she could help my mom find a place to stay in Baton Rouge for the rest of the year. Pearl had money and loved my mom. Toni already begged me to stay with her. When I finished school, I could get a full-time job. After making enough money, I'd find a place where we all could live, and bring Mom back here. It'd be hard on me but a lot harder on my mom. I got two days to get us packed and out of there. We had lunch at her cottage house and got

Toni back to work a little late. I finished my walk back to my truck, which wouldn't be mine for long.

Written while in Hospital

Chapter 20

I was awakened in my hospital bed, by loud voices and hectic commotion. I slowly opened my eyes to see the large rectangular fluorescent light fixture above my bed. I could hear sobbing and other voices. My vision was a little misty and obscured my peripheral vision. Suddenly, close to my face, I see a pair of beautiful green eyes sparkling with moisture. A huge tear drop fell from one of the emerald eyes and landed on my cheek. I smiled and feebly said, "Brenda". She kissed me softly, then the darkness took me away.

Copied from spiral notebooks

Chapter 21

When I got home, I went into the workshop. Leaning against the bench, I shook my head knowing that everything was too heavy to take with me. Losing everything. Maybe I needed to flush everything and start again, with a woman like Toni, starting again would be kind of easy. As I walked up the back steps, I could see muddy footprints coming in and going out. Looking back behind me, I could see where several people had crossed from the back lot to here, walking in the mud. At the top of the stairs, I saw the kitchen door was opened. In the kitchen, more muddy footprints. I didn't step in any of the footprints but hurried up to my mother's bedroom, shouting out her name. She lay in her bed, her eyes wide-opened, staring intensely at the ceiling. Her nightgown, bed sheets, and mattress soaked in her blood. The arms were stretched out as if two people were still holding her down. The nightgown was ripped open, exposing her ample breast.

And in between her breast was a huge gaping wound with red meat and white bone hanging out. Blood was still slowly dripping out of the wound and splattering blood trails of casted off blood impacting the headboard, wall, and ceiling. My mom was staring intently at her own blood.

I fell to my knees, my racked body shaking. Tears so big, they blurred my vision. I wailed and then screamed at the top of my lungs. I instantly became silent as the vomit poured out of me and the dry heaves gagged me. Struggling for breath, I felt the darkness slithering up around me. "No, NO!"

"STOP!" I commanded myself, "STOP!" I restrained the shaking.

With all the strength in my body, more than I ever even knew I had, I stopped the impending seizure that would have incapacitated me from helping my mom. I pulled off my shirt and wiped the vomit, snot, and tears from my face. On shaky knees, I stood and knowing that this would be the last time I will see her, told my mommy I love her. Slowly stepping out of the room and careful to not step in the muddy tracks, I made it to the phone in the living room. On the center hub of the rotary dial was a new thing that Fannie read about and cut out of the newspaper. It fits behind the clear plastic hub, the numbers nine-one-one. I dialed it and told the pleasant-sounding woman that my mother had just been murdered.

In three minutes, a police officer was there, in five, another one appeared. In ten minutes, an ambulance and a fire truck showed up. About fifteen minutes later, Chief Detective Hansen, hat in hand, was standing with me in the front yard. He looked like he was going to break down and sob. I had told the first officer on the scene everything and helped him write it all down. Chief Detective Hansen held that report in his hands and had just finished reading it. He also had just returned from viewing the crime scene.

"Miles, I am so horrified by this, it's hard for me to speak to you right now, I am literally about to break down. Please forgive me, son, I'm trying to be strong and do my job, Miles, I'm so sorry." With that, he put his hand on my shoulder and his forehead on that hand and tried to suppress his whimpering. That made me feel good when he said "son." I thanked him for all he had done. He used the ever-present handkerchief in his suit pocket to wipe his tears and nose. He wiped mine too.

As we both pulled ourselves together, Detective Hansen solemnly asked me if I knew anything about who had done this. His tone of voice was low and strained, he said it while looking at his shoes. Without hesitation, I explained that this was directly part of what I'd already told him. I then told him that big bad Brad's gang was the main supplier of illegal drugs and stolen cigarettes and alcohol at the high school. I'd been extorted by him for years, to give him answers on tests and finals. He had threatened Candi, my family, and friends. His problem killed Trevor – I wondered if Trevor was stabbed in the heart. Big Bad Brad had planted false evidence in my locker and told the school's narc to bust me. I lost my scholarship to Big Bad Brad. He knew where I lived and that I should have been home. I should have been murdered there, not my mom. Chief Detective Hansen had to ask me where I was this morning and afternoon. I told him about my trip to the bank, then lunch with Toni, and the phone call to my mom from the diner. The Chief Detective said that the house would be sealed for at least a week during the investigation. He said I'd have access to the house and I could take out anything I wanted. The coroner would be there for a while so Chief Detective Hansen asked me to go to the station and give my statement. He told me that Toni had tried to call me. I could talk to her when I'm there.

After giving my police interview and signing my statement, Toni gave me her key and said she would be home by five. She held me tight, whispered in my ear that she loved my mom just as much as she loves me. She'd do anything for me forever. She squeezed the stuffing out of me then kissed me hard and told me to be careful! No one knew about our relationship so I was sure nothing would happen to either of us.

After a shower, I laid naked in Toni's big brass bed and knew what I had to do. In the years to come, Toni would understand.

The next morning, I went home for the last time. All the doors were locked but I had the key. Check marks and circles were drawn on the floor around the muddy footprints. Arrows indicated direction of movement. I didn't look in my mom's room. Inside my closet, up above the wooden doorframe, was a niche formed by the header and the wall's frame. I hid money there to use to buy engines and parts; the auto scrapers only dealt in cash. I surprised myself with how much was there. I hoped it was enough to cremate my mom and bury the ashes in my father's plot. Toni would get it in her mail in a couple of days.

Standing there in my room, I could remember good times and bad. All the things I had collected and made. My desk with its worn edges and chipped wood. Files upon files that were so important to me. The view from my window, Old Hank sneaking over to the Gomez sisters' house. The mattress I'd been sleeping on for, well, forever, I guess. Candi's strong naked body on top of me. I sat on my bed and cried for some time, then hauled my sorry ass up and grabbed some clean underwear, socks, and my best western shirt. My cowboy boots, the handmade, laced leather belt with a silver buckle. And finally, the new Levi boot-cut jeans, all of which I folded and stuffed in a Navy surplus duffle bag. I stood just outside my bedroom and looked down the hallway. Never noticed how the carpet runner was so worn, or the pictures on the walls of my sister and I at different stages of our lives. I felt like I was a hundred years old. Each step down this hallway was a memory of my past, and a valid path for my future.

With the kitchen door locked behind me forever, I entered my machine shop. The crunch of dirt and gravel underfoot and the smell of oil and grease was all so familiar to me. It made me feel so sad. I came here for a reason, get on with it, damn it!

Pulling and shifting my big rolling toolbox, I exposed a bundle of discarded oily rags. Inside these oily rags was my dad's Smith & Wesson Model 36, .38 Chief's Special with a four-inch barrel. On the wall right by the double barn doors, hung my coveralls, and underneath the coveralls was my work coat. My dad was not a tall man. As a matter of fact, my mom was just a little taller than him. My dad wore a Levi Sherpa-lined trucker jacket, 38 M. He wore a suit and tie to work every day, but wore his Levi jeans and jacket on the weekends. I was a little kid when he wore it as we worked in the yard and around the house. I now could fit in my dad's jacket and it concealed the gun rig very well. The shoulder holster was rolled up inside the jacket. I put on the holster and tightened the chest strap, then the jacket. I had practiced with the gun and holster and had fired all but six rounds. I could reach into the jacket, grab the gun's butt, and have the gun in front of me in a shooter's stance in two seconds. The chest strap had six little leather loops to slide extra bullets in and all six were occupied. I performed a quick draw and held it. Slowly lowering my arm, I surveyed all my work and accomplishments in such a short amount of time.

We all make sacrifices for our family and the ones we love. Sometimes those sacrifices demand a grievous ending. If those greedy bankers want my truck, they'll have to come and get it. I had a few errands to run, then prepare dinner for Toni and me.

Copied from spiral notebooks

Chapter 22

Early the next morning, I kissed Toni goodbye as she hurried out the door so she wouldn't be late. I showered, dressed in the western clothes I took from my house, then I drove to school for my first day back from suspension.

I had parked in the student parking lot close to big bad Brad's four-wheel drive van. I knew that Brad went to the locker room first thing in the morning. By the end of first period, he would walk out the locker room's double door heading to his first morning class. Which would be in about ten minutes. Sacrifice.

From the parking lot, I walked up the sidewalk to the back entries of the auditorium. Rounding the corner of the auditorium, I walked through the breezeway to the entrance of the boys' and girls' locker rooms. Through the double door and into the four-way intersection of the human highway. I came in from the stadium entrance, to my left was the hallway to the boys' locker room, and to my right was the girls'. Dead ahead of me was the stairway up to the gymnasium. There were very few people walking around but the bell was going to ring any minute.

And so it did. A river of people spilled out of the locker rooms while others were pouring in. Within a couple minutes, the crowd thinned out and I heard the rebel yell just before I saw big bad Brad coming out the double doors with Frank in tow. I was standing by the girls' locker room doors and took a couple of steps toward Brad. He saw me and broke out with a half-smile and the thumb hooked in his jeans' pockets. He titled his head back and started laughing. A late crowd of girls leaving the locker room cut me off as they headed out to the stadium. Big bad Brad would never stop destroying everything I loved and cherished until I was dead. If he found out about Toni and me, she could be in danger. Even if I killed Brad, this wouldn't guarantee Toni's safety with the size and scope of this criminal enterprise. But with the death of big bad Brad and myself, it would halt any other retaliatory action. My death would stop the violence happening to the people around me. Toni would get my letter explaining all of this, and the money to bury my mother.

As soon as the crowd of girls passed me, I saw a guy who just came down the stairway then turned the corner right in front of Brad. Just at that second, the air was ripped apart with a gunshot. Big bad Brad dropped like a bag of potatoes. Another gunshot – Frank didn't have a chance. He had tried to turn back to the locker room but erupted into a red mist. Shattering my eardrums.

By this time, I had taken ten steps forward and now stood a good two feet from big bad Brad's sprawled body. The shooter, not seeing me, stepped up to Frank and executed him with a bullet to the brain. The blast offset my equilibrium. The shooter slowly turned till he was looking right in my eyes. I remembered this guy, he was the stoner who sat in the quad and listened to Candi playing the violin. I couldn't believe how bad he looked, his white pasty skin and missing teeth, thinning hair. The sores on his face were red with scabs, his wild eyes sunken deeply in his skull. I glared at his glassy stare. Then I saw his right eye twitch. My hand was already grabbing the butt of the Smith & Wesson Model 36, .38 Chief's Special when he discharged his first round which was real low; he fired way too soon. I had the gun out, up and pointed at his chest, when he fired the second round which was way too wide, but I did hear the bullet go by my head. I continued to apply pressure to the trigger when the pistol bucked in my hand and the blast sent shockwaves instantly though my body. My ears were ringing loudly because of the enclosed space. The junky dropped his gun, grabbed his chest and let out a blooded, gurgling cough, the blood splashing on the floor in front of him. The junky fell to his knees and took a watery breath, then fell flat on his face. A mournful groan attracted my attention. Looking down at my feet, I saw Big Bad Brad's half smile was traded for the look of horror.

"I can't feel my legs," he cried.

What was going on? I couldn't believe what just happened. There must have been a lot of people out there who hated Brad as much as I did. I lowered my arm and stared at Brad. I guess I felt sorry for him.

A calm and concerned voice called my name. Coach Vargas was right behind me, telling me everything was fine. He was saying that it was all over and that I should put the gun on the ground. People were everywhere, from the coaches' offices and the gymnasium; they all heard the gunfire and followed the sound. I set the gun down and Coach Vargas walked me to his office. He sat me down and said, "I saw what you did, Miles, you saved us from that manic with a gun. You saved us." And with that, he told me to stay right here and ran out of the office. I'd failed. I was still alive. I hadn't saved anyone! With my head in my hands, I pondered my next move, what could I do. Go to jail for the rest of my life?!

Principle Gerber burst into the office, he was so mad that he couldn't get the words out of his mouth.

"How could you do this, what have you done!?" is all that I could understand as he stamped his feet, knocking things off the desk and screaming hysterically. He kicked a desk, slipped, and fell to the floor. As he struggled to get up, he started crying. I felt so bad for him. Coach Vargas helped him up and out of the office. All the students were taken out of the gymnasium and the locker rooms emptied. No one touched the bodies, although Brad was taken to the hospital by an ambulance. The police arrived. The two officers said nothing to me and posed as guards around the scene. When backup was provided, the first officer on the scene scooped me up and dumped me in an interrogation room, at the Unified Police Station.

They took my shoes, belt, and coat. They frowned at me when they saw my shoulder holster. I handed that over as well. I was left in there for over an hour. A young detective came in and asked me some personal questions like name, address, phone number and so on. After the questions, I asked some of my own, like what was next – no answer. Could I talk to Chief Detective Hansen? no answer. Can I have a drink of water? After ten minutes, he brought me a Big Red cream soda; I don't like cream soda. They had taken my father's watch so I had no reference of time. I had to knock on the door to let someone know that I had to go to the bathroom. Chief Detective Hansen leaned in and gestured for me to follow him. We silently walked out of the squad room and down the hall to the women's bathroom. The Chief Detective looked at me and put his index finger to his lips, then shouted, "Cleaning." No one answered so he shuffled me inside. I ran to one of the stalls and quieted my bladder. I could hear Chief Detective Hansen washing his hands. When I exited the stall, Chief Detective Hansen was leaning against the sink, arms crossed on his chest, and staring at the floor. Chief Detective Hansen, without raising his head, told me not to say a word. He said that a few people were pulling for me. He told me not to admit to anything. To keep my mouth shut and my ears open. The two boys were dead. Brad had a bullet lodged in his lower spine. The doctors couldn't operate on him, it was too risky. Chief Detective Hansen wanted me to spend the night in the interrogation room and see a judge tomorrow morning. There were blankets, a cot, and officers there twenty-four hours a day for whatever I needed. The door would be kept unlocked. The Chief Detective didn't want to put me in jail, and this was the best he could do. He stood up, pointed at me and said, "Stay." And walked around the privacy wall and out the door.

A minute later, the door burst open and Toni ran around the wall jumping up on me, wrapped her arms and legs around me crying.

Stepping backward, I leaned against the sinks and held on to her. "Chief Detective Hansen said when this is over, we can go wherever we want and start over again. Oh, Miles, tell me you love me. Tell me you want to marry me. Oh, Miles, I think I'm pregnant." She started crying again, I couldn't understand anything she was saying so I just agreed with whatever she said. Chief Detective Hansen broke us up and sent Toni back to work. We walked back to the interrogation room where a cot and blankets were waiting for me. A sergeant had bought me two Whataburgers, some fries, and a chocolate shake. Like a condemned man's last meal, I ate slowly and appreciated every bite. I occupied myself with a handful of old Hot Rod magazines and a deck of cards.

In the morning, I was taken to the locker room where the police officers could shower and change into their uniforms. I showered, borrowed a razor and shaving cream then dressed in the western clothes I wore yesterday. Back in the squad room, I was taken to Chief Detective Hansen's office. The Chief Detective was working feverishly on his IBM Selectric electric typewriter. He told me we needed to hurry up and wait, so sit down and shut up.

That afternoon, a telephone call sent us to the fifth floor. This was where all of the department managers' offices were, and the Chief of Police. Which was the place I found myself in. Chief Barnhill met us at the wooden double doors of his office and ushered us in. Inside his office was Judge Covarrubias, the School District's Superintendent, and Principal Gerber, all seated awaiting our arrival. Also in attendance was a host of other bald-headed and gray-haired old men. All of whom saw me as either friend or foe.

Judge Covarrubias sat at the Chief's desk and I was brought to a chair placed right in front of that desk. The Judge had deeply furrowed wrinkles on his face. His hair grew from behind the ears in a ring around the back of his head. His small beady eyes casting an icy stare directly at me. The Chief introduced everyone. There were lawyers, district attorneys, and a representative of the governor's office.

After all the niceties, the Judge got down to business. "We," the Judge said, waving his hand at the people in the room, "have talked this whole affair over and have a proposition for you." The Judge said this while organizing several pages of paper. "First, I hereby find you guilty of carrying a loaded and concealed weapon." The Judge saw my reaction to that in my eyes. "Wait a minute, hear me out now, with that weapon you shot and killed one Gary Kerns in self-defense. We view that shooting as justifiable homicide. Mr. Kerns had on his person several loaded magazines that could have been used to kill a lot of people. We feel that is what Mr. Kerns had planned to do. For that, all of us in this room agree that all charges against you are rescinded. We have prepared a pardon exonerating you from any crime in the past to this date. All we need is your signature and your guarantee that you will leave this county and never return." I turned to look at Principal Gerber who shook his head and looked at the floor.

The school's superintendent bellowed out, "You've been expelled from school!"

"Your family's home has been foreclosed on." This was said by one of the lawyers.

"Your family's in Pleasant Hills now, resting." This came from the governor's representative.

"There's nothing left for you here," the Judge had made the final comment. I asked if I could read the pardon. While I was occupied, everyone else lit a cigarette or cigar and poured from the bar a brandy, bourbon, or gin. The pardon was everything the Judge said it was. An absolute pardon for any act to this date. They couldn't wait to sweep this under the rug and get rid of me, just like what they did to my father. The Governor had already signed the document. The space for a witness signature was for the judge, then my signature. I asked for a xerox of the pardon. When the two documents were on the desk and in good order, I unceremoniously signed both copies. The Judge followed suit and handed me my copy. The Judge picked up all the other files off the Chief of Police's desk and added them to his copy of the pardon. He put everything in his briefcase and turned to leave. And then it just came out of my mouth!

"I wonder how many of you are making money in the drug trade," I said loudly. That sucked all the air out of the room. Everyone froze. The look of guilt was on all of their faces. "Don't worry, the Federal Police will be investigating this very soon and all of you will pay."

"You've been deceased, punk, no one will listen to you!" the Judge yelled this with his eyeballs bulging.

"When the auto salvage yards burned down, you guys lost a lot of cash. That's where you hide it before cleaning it with the bank's help," I said this right to the Judge's face. "I didn't save anyone, I was there to kill big bad Brad. He is a murderer and a drug dealer. I was going to crush him like the cockroach he is." Everyone forgot their smokes and drinks, grabbed their briefcases and headed out the huge wooden double doors. I suddenly realized these were the same type of doors in the Vice President's office at the bank. They must have cost a small fortune. The banning and hinges were hand forged out of wrought iron, while the door's handle and key way plate look as though they belonged in a castle. All purchased from blood money.

"Hansen!" the Chief of Police screamed. "Escort this person out of the building, we'll have nothing more to do with him, god damn it!" Chief Detective Hansen took me to the property room to reclaim my things. My wallet and jacket was all I recovered, the gun and holster wouldn't be returned. I didn't want them anyway. Chief Detective Hansen walked with me trying to give me some advice and some money he had saved. The advice I took, but the money I respectfully declined. As we entered the reception area, Toni saw me. She ran around the tall desk and hugged me. I told her they dropped all the charges, but I had to go away. The Governor wanted me to leave the state. She looked at Chief Detective Hansen, he was shaking his head.

"I'll quit," she said bravely. "Let me get my purse and coat."

As she went around the desk, I heard a loud voice yell, "HEY, YOU!"

Chief Detective Hansen and I both turned at the same time to see a tall, broad-shouldered, uniformed officer moving quickly toward us, from the way we just came.

Chief Detective Hansen held up his hand and shouted, "Sergeant Kozlowski, get back to your station!" The big bad sergeant easily pushed Chief Detective Hansen out of the way.

He stopped just two feet from me. "You were going to KILL my boy!" Big bad Brad's last name was Kozlowski, this must have been his father. I was getting tired of all this shit.

"It's too bad I didn't get the chance." And with that said, I started to turn toward Toni when the gun blast knocked me to the floor. The blood squished out of me like a wet sponge.

Looking up from the floor, I could see Toni coming to me in slow motion. Her purse was falling from her shoulder, her arms stretched out toward me. The next blast hit her in the chest, pushing her back against the tall reception desk. Her ruined chest and vacant eyes told me everything I needed to know. My Toni is gone, and I'd soon follow. Two consecutive gunshots rang out, I turned my head and looked painfully over my shoulder. Chief Detective Hansen had shot Sergeant Kozlowski twice at point blank range. Sergeant Kozlowski simultaneously fired once at Chief Detective Hansen, blowing him back into the wall. He slid down and landed into a reception chair. Chief Detective Hansen and Sargent Kozlowski continued to fire at each other till the detective dropped his gun and slumped over, and the sergeant fell forward.

The sergeant and I were both flat on the floor, right next to each other. I could see his eyes fading in and out, like when a small child is falling asleep in the high chair. Suddenly his eyes focused on me. His face scrunched up and he slowly and strenuously pointed the gun at me. The gun was a huge, chrome monstrosity. He was having trouble holding it steady. With my working arm, I slowly wrapped my fingers and thumb around the barrel and steadied it, pointing it directly at my head. This seemed to have pissed him off, for he put newfound strength in his trigger finger. The hammer slowly drew back, until…click.

The firing pin struck a spent cartridge. Damn. This was the second time I tried to kill myself and failed. The gun flopped over and Sergeant Kozlowski took his last labored breath. Lucky guy. I distinctly remembered the coppery metallic smell of the small river of blood trickling down the linoleum floor. There wasn't much of my blood in that river. The hospital staff told me that my dad's Levi Sherpa lined trucker's jacket held my large chest wound closed, preventing me from bleeding to death. Lucky me.

Written while in Hospital

Chapter 23

So here I am, with no idea how long I've been laying in this hospital bed. I'm not sleeping, it's more like passing out from the pain. It feels like someone has built a campfire on my chest. My legs and groin are inflamed and swollen to double the normal size. They put me in traction so I could be lifted off the bed and my bedsore can be drained, covered in Vaseline and bandage. It's even more painful than the campfire on my chest. I can only write for a few minutes at a time because of my trembling from the cold sweats. I'm wearing an oxygen mask to help fight off the bacterial infection in my blood. I take short quick breaths because my one lung fills up very rapidly. The pain medication makes me groggy.

Several times I've come to and saw the little orderly kneeling at my bedside. Her forehead resting against her folded hands, praying and whimpering at the same time. I'm so dehydrated, I can't cry. No one needs to tell me that I'm dying. My handwriting is probably hard to read.

But something woke me up. I feel no pain. The medical machines are silent. It must be night because there is darkness all around me. Above me is the large rectangle light. The light is blue like the sky. I can see wispy clouds floating by. I am startled when something swiftly passes across the sky blue light. And again, two more darts by.

Then a whole bunch of – why, there are black birds flying by! They're so beautiful with their yellow eyes. The darkness around me is deep and formidable. But the sky blue light above me feels so warm and happy! I can see something emerging from the edge of the sky blue light, it looks like curly blonde hair. The forehead. Then the eyes peek over. My sister, her laughing face pokes over the edge.

"Hurry up, pumpkin head," she hollered and laughed. That's what she used to call me.

A shadow appears over the edge, the blue light hits his face, my father, oh my! He smiles and says, "Welcome home, son."

Then another face, my mom, Oh Mommy. "Love you, sweety," she says with her movie star looks and bright white teeth, she is so beautiful.

Then the Gomez sisters with the same hair-do and hat, but I still can tell them apart. Old Hank with his seldom smile. Detective Hansen, nodding his head, "You did good boy," he said while tipping his hat.

And then Toni, oh Toni, her beautiful light blue eyes shining bright. I'm crying so hard. I reach up for them. Hey, both my arms work. I just want to grab them and hug them all. The light is so warm and BRIGHT.

Publisher's note: The final paragraph in the last spiral notebook was illegible and indecipherable. Because of poor handwriting, pencil smudging, smear, and faded paper, it is perceived that speculating the contents would not be in the reader's interest. Because of these complications it is believed that this is the story's end.

www.ingramcontent.com/pod-product-compliance
Lightning Source LLC
Chambersburg PA
CBHW062040240125
20821CB00007B/81